THE LEAN RIDER

THE LEAN RIDER

Cliff Farrell

GUNSMOKE

First published in the US by Doubleday

This hardback edition 2011
by AudioGO Ltd
by arrangement with
Golden West Literary Agency

ISBN 978 1 445 85680 3

British Library Cataloguing in Publication Data available.

Printed and bound in Great Britain by
MPG Books Group Limited

CHAPTER 1

Lisa Randolph clung to the seat of the spring wagon as it lurched over the rough trail. The route was a meandering wheel track that labored through hills coated with brush and low, durable trees. Here and there were natural clearings.

The trees were of a kind unfamiliar to her. They bore thorns. They were mesquite, but she did not know that nor, at the moment, did she care. The thickets were also armed with spikes, and their foliage was shockingly alien to her and hostile.

She kept telling herself that she would turn back if it were possible. She felt that there was no chance of retreat now. The truth was that there was within her a stern sense of obligation which was forcing her to go through with this. She had given a promise. It was pride that drove her, even though she would not admit the truth of that even to herself. How could there be pride in a woman who had agreed to make such a long journey to marry a man she had seen only once, and then only for a few hours?

Her arms were numb from the effort of retaining her place in the vehicle. An apathy was settling upon her. It did not matter now. Nothing mattered. The distance she had traveled to reach this land of thorned growth seemed to stretch endlessly back to the orderly life she had led among her own kind in Chicago. Orderly, yes. But dispiriting.

First there had been the journey by train to St. Louis and the steamboat trip to New Orleans. That had been pleasant enough, for she had been buoyed by the shining newness of the adventure.

After that, a stormy voyage in sail to a port named Galveston and a hot and crowded stagecoach trip from Houston to San Antonio. Another and shabbier stage, drawn by wild Spanish mules, had brought her, after an overnight ordeal, to a settlement named San Ysidro.

And now, on this day in April, 1871, she was riding in this rented vehicle, a mere box on wheels which was barely large enough for her and a few pieces of her luggage and the man she had hired to drive her to her destination.

1

"Can this be I?" The words had kept drifting through her mind with increasing despair these past few days. She must have spoken them aloud, for the driver turned and peered at her inquiringly. He was an angular man with a prominent nose. He had a high forehead and mild brown eyes and a thin, scrubby brown mustache. He wore a flat-brimmed black hat, somewhat in the Quaker fashion, but he was no Quaker, for beneath his rusty black coat was strapped a holstered cap and ball pistol. A muzzle-loading shotgun lay on the wagon floor between his dog-eared boots. He smelled faintly of alcoholic spirits and cloves.

His name was Jones—Micah Jones. He was well educated and had courtly manners. She had heard him addressed as "Professor" in San Ysidro. She had guessed that he was a schoolteacher, but when she had asked him about it she had touched on a tender spot. "I did some tutoring in my early days," he had admitted gruffly. "But not in Texas. Teaching's a female prerogative. I'm a cattle hand. I work mainly at Bar B."

Evidently he was an understanding man, for he did not press the subject when she offered no explanation of the thought she had voiced aloud. Instead he said, "Nice afternoon! Hot and dry for this early in spring."

"Yes." Lisa added nothing more. She appreciated his choice of the classic generality, the weather, as a topic of comment. She knew that he must be achingly curious about her, just as she had been conscious of the wave of interest that had stirred the residents of San Ysidro after she had alighted at the stage station.

No one would ever know the utter desolation that had come upon her as she had stood on the dusty clay sidewalk alongside her baggage, gazing at San Ysidro. She had been mentally picturing a tree-shaded community of mellowed buildings, with fine carriages at the curbs.

The reality was a scatter of flat-topped structures at a sun-baked crossroads, with half a dozen mongrel dogs in full cry as the stagecoach rattled away, leaving her there in her aloneness.

Three lean horses with wicked eyes, bearing saddles that seemed far too big for them, had been tied before a place the name of which, according to a faded painted sign over the door, was the Mud Turtle. The Mud Turtle evidently was a saloon, and Lisa had been very careful not to look toward it any oftener than was necessary.

Many of the buildings in the town were constructed of what seemed to be mud-colored bricks faced with whitewashed plaster. Lisa had never heard of adobe. She had stood in this strange place gazing around, hoping that Frank O'Hara would appear and claim her. But that had not occurred. She had hardly expected such good fortune, for there had been no way of apprising him of the exact time of her arrival in this land of uncertain communication.

She had inquired of the stage agent as to where she might locate Mr. O'Hara. She had been aware that his curiosity had almost gotten out of hand to the point of asking direct questions. But native reticence had prevailed. She was beginning to value highly the custom of this region which forbade inquiry into a stranger's past, his future or his present intentions.

She wanted no past to remember and no future to think about. As for the present—it was to be faced soon. Sitting in the spring wagon, she fought the increasing panic that was causing her legs to quiver beneath the many-petticoated traveling dress she wore.

The vehicle rounded a turn and she winced and averted her eyes. The shrunken, mummified forms of a score or more of cattle were scattered over an expanse of sun-cracked yellow surface alongside the road, which evidently had been a mud flat in the recent past.

Micah Jones spoke. "Some of Frank's Triangle O cattle."

"Mr. O'Hara's?"

Micah nodded. "His T O stock ranges south of here mainly. These drifted during a storm last winter and bogged down. Nobody passed by on the trail for a couple of days because of the weather. After that it was too late. They were all she stuff."

"She stuff?"

He looked at her, puzzled. "Cows, ma'am. Female animals. The most of 'em were in calf. They . . ."

Lisa's expression halted him. She sat rigid. As a proper lady should, she pretended she had not heard.

He eyed her disbelievingly. "What I mean, ma'am, is that . . ."

"I'm sure I understand," Lisa said hastily.

They drove on in silence for a time. "It seems odd that so many animals could have strayed without Mr. O'Hara discovering their absence," Lisa commented.

When Micah made no response to that she went on, "The death of those cows must have been quite a loss to him."

Micah laughed—a trifle cynically, she thought. "Loss?" he said. "There're plenty more cows."

"That's a cruel thing to say," Lisa remonstrated.

He shrugged. "About the only thing cattle are worth around here are their hides and tallow. Ranchers are going busted."

"Then there actually are other persons living in this—this wilderness?" Lisa asked.

Micah answered a trifle testily. "Quite a number. But more than there will be before summer's ended. The Barbee outfit, for one, is pulling out. They're gathering their brand and are going to move north, lock, stock and barrel, and find new country somewhere."

"Barbee?" Lisa repeated. "Mr. O'Hara mentioned that name in a letter. Neighbors, I believe."

Micah nodded. "We'll hit the Barbee place about three miles ahead. Their place is called Monte Vista. O'Hara House— that's Frank's place—is only a couple of miles farther on. I reckon you'll enjoy meeting Hester Barbee."

"A woman, I take it?" Lisa asked.

Micah chuckled. "That I'll guarantee. Hester's the woman-est woman you'll ever meet. She's the mother of the two Barbee boys. She'll take you under wing like a mother hen."

Lisa stiffened inwardly, determined to be independent of this particular mothering person.

After a time Micah cleared his throat and ventured his first direct question. "You a relative of Frank's?"

Lisa had a moment of satisfaction. Apparently no one knew the purpose of her arrival. At least Frank O'Hara was not a talkative man. "No," she said.

That ended the conversation. There was only the grind of the wheels and the scuffle of the team's hooves while Micah contemplated the wreckage of his inquisitiveness.

Presently he straightened in the seat, peering. Lisa became aware of crashing sounds in the brush. These came rapidly closer. She heard pounding hooves and the grunting of ani-mals laboring under great stress.

A wild, screeching shout that hardly sounded human arose in the thickets. Lisa had heard that Indians were still to be reckoned with in this wild land. She gazed at Micah in alarm.

"Easy, ma'am," he said. "That's nothing to be afraid of. It's only a brush popper rounding up Barbee stock."

An animal burst from the chaparral a distance away and came racing toward the wagon. Lisa stared, shocked. To her, all bovines came under the general classification of peace-ful ruminants, lying in green meadows, chewing their cuds.

This creature seemed from another world. It had powerful, sharp-tipped horns spreading as wide as a man could reach. It was the color of brown suede and its eyes had the green-ish shine of pure fury. It moved with the springy, lithe stride of a wild animal and its whistling breathing was a savage sound. It was a Longhorn steer.

A horseman appeared from the brush in pursuit. His aspect was as startling as that of his quarry. He rode low in the saddle, hugging the neck of his horse, his hat jammed well down, a leather-cuffed arm shielding his face from thorned branches. He yelled again—the high-pitched, primitive sound that had frightened Lisa. The fierce, challenging shout of the hunter.

The steer was heading toward the wagon. Micah leaped to his feet, waving his arms and whooping. The animal broke stride and whirled to dart in another direction. That was its undoing. The pursuer was upon it. Lisa saw the falcon dart of a looped rope. In the next instant the steer was yanked sidewise to land on its flank with a violence that brought a gasp of sympathy from her.

The rider left the saddle and raced down the rope, hand over hand. He carried a shorter length of rope in his teeth. He threw himself bodily on the steer and in seconds of concentrated activity bound its legs securely. It was all done so swiftly Lisa did not realize what was happening.

The hunter lay back, using the heaving body of the breathless animal as a support, and looked up at them in the wagon. He blew from laboring lungs. "Double damn his o'nery hide!" he wheezed. "I got him at last."

A trickle of blood coursed down his cheek where a thorned branch had raked his skin. Gore also showed on a barked knuckle. His hat, brush-snagged and faded by weather, was lashed down tightly by a braided leather chin strap. Its wide brim was bent to the contours of his head, and Lisa understood that it served as a partial shield for his features during his reckless plunging through the brush.

Those features were lean and ruggedly molded. He had very dark hair and dark straight brows. His eyes were dark also, but they were eyes that were alive—very much alive. He looked at her boldly, as though estimating her weight and age.

He wore a jacket made of heavy leather which bore the marks of long use in the thickets. He had heavy leather leggings buckled to his thighs. He was dusty and in need of a shave. His hair had not seen a barber's shears in weeks. His horse still retained patches of its winter's coat. It also wore leather, in the shape of a heavy breast-apron which protected it to its knees.

"Muy bueno, Micah," he said, his lungs still laboring. "If you hadn't turned that bunch quitter I'd still be bustin' brush on his tail."

"Abel," Micah said, and his manner was suddenly as formal as though they were standing on a polished floor, "I want to present you to Miss Elizabeth Randolph. Miss Randolph, this is Abel Barbee."

Abel Barbee got to his feet, loosened the chin strap and removed his hat. Lisa judged him to be in the late twenties. He was well above medium height and there was power in his shoulders. But above all he gave the impression of being a person who made his own decisions and was ready to stand by them.

He continued his unhurried way of sizing her up. Lisa endured this inspection and felt embarrassed color rising all over her. She sensed that he resented her. She wondered if it could be her garb. The little bright festoon of blue ribbon that had adorned her poke bonnet was drooping now, shaken partly from its moorings by days of jolting wheeled travel, its sprightliness faded by sun and dust. The long linen duster she wore over her dress was shapeless and of a neutral hue.

Abel Barbee's glance swung to the portmanteau and the carpetbag and two hatboxes which were lashed to the scant afterdeck of the small wagon. He seemed to disapprove of these items also.

"No'therna?" he inquired.

He evidently was a very truculent person. Lisa did not answer his brash question. "How do you do, Mr. Barbee!" she said with strict formality.

"No'therna, shore enough," Abel Barbee said.

"Miss Randolph comes from Chicago," Micah Jones said. "She wants to get in touch with Frank O'Hara. I'm driving her out to O'Hara House."

Abel Barbee was frowning. Lisa sat primly gazing off into the distance, ignoring him. She was determined to let him flounder in his own curiosity before she would offer a word of explanation. Suddenly, intuitively, she sensed that he knew why she was here. She looked at him quickly. And then she was sure. Once again she felt warmth sweep over her and into her face. This continued as Abel Barbee's critical inspection of her went on.

Her fingers, slim and well cared for, were tightly locked together in her lap. She resisted the desire to smooth her skirt and tuck into place a strand of her hair which had crept from beneath the band of the bonnet. It was becoming hair of a deep golden, coppery hue. She was a slender young woman of twenty-four, made thinner of face by the doubts and anxieties of these past months, but obviously of excellent figure. Her eyes were a fine, warm shade of gray. She was well-bred and trained in the ways of social grace. This background was very evident in her demeanor. She carried her needlework in her reticule for moments when there was opportunity for idle hands, and she had always turned away from violence or vulgarity.

Abel Barbee's inspection went on for seconds and the silence deepened. He finally spoke. "You better stop by Monte Vista an' let Hester handle this, Micah."

The way he said it brought a chill of apprehension to Lisa. She saw a glance pass between the two men.

"I'd already planned on doing that," Micah said. He paused, then added, "So that's how it is?"

Abel Barbee shrugged. "I had counted on Frank helpin' us round up. An' you too, Micah. You could have pitched in, instead of settin' around a tequila jug in San Ysidro."

"I will," Micah said hastily. "I will, Abel. I'll start riding in the morning."

"I hoped to be trailin' no'th days ago," Abel said wearily. "But here we are, still poppin' knotheads out'n the tules."

He kicked the supine steer in the stomach with the toe of his boot. The animal grunted, rolled its eyes and tried vainly to rise.

Lisa started to voice a protest at punishing a helpless animal, then decided to let it pass. It had not been a vigorous action, in any event, and was utterly without rancor. It had been more the effort of a discouraged, disgruntled man.

"I wish you'd busted your cussed neck," Abel said to the steer.

He spoke to Micah. "Got to lid-sew him. We've had him in the bunch twice an' he high-tailed it away into the shinnery each time. Wore out two horses an' myself runnin' him today. You kin help choke him down."

"All right," Micah said. He placed the reins of the team in Lisa's surprised hands and leaped to the ground. She sat rigid and a little frightened. She had handled carriage horses and had ridden sidesaddle on bridle paths. But those horses had been gentle. This team of roans, like all the animals she had seen in this region, were wild and unpredictable.

Abel walked to his mount, freed the lariat and tossed a loop around the steer's neck. He handed the rope to Micah. "Squeeze him tight when I'm ready," he said.

He removed the heavy leather brush coat and the leather cuffs. He wore a gingham shirt in a distinctive blue and white check pattern. Lisa was surprised. In a land where gray homespun, striped hickory and dyed linsey were almost universal attire, gingham was a refreshing novelty, especially for masculine wear. Evidently the Barbees were a cut or two above average.

He heaped together a few twigs and a wisp of dry leaves, used flint and steel on a prepared wick of cotton "punk," and soon had a small fire burning. From his saddle he brought a short length of iron with a curved end, which he placed to heat.

"Might as well road-brand him while I got him," he said.

He produced a small packet and from it fished a needle and thread. For a time he was occupied in breathless concentration, attempting to slip the tongue-wet thread through the elusive eye of the needle. Lisa ached to speed this task but decided that he was the sort of a person who would resent interference, particularly from a female, and a northerner at that.

Finally he succeeded. He straddled the neck of the steer. "Clamp down on the old rockhead, Micah," he commanded.

He bent close and began working. The steer uttered an outraged snort and began to struggle. Micah dug in his heels and squeezed as directed. The steer, its breath reduced, subsided with a sigh.

Abel Barbee calmly resumed his task. Suddenly Lisa realized what was going on. She came to her feet with a horrified gasp. Hurriedly she wrapped the reins around the whipsocket. Gathering her skirts, she leaped from the wagon and descended upon the two men, petticoats swishing.

"Stop that!" she commanded. "Stop that this instant!"

Abel Barbee paused, needle poised, looking up at her in amazement. "Stop what?"

Lisa bent closer to make sure that what she had suspected was true. It was. She felt nausea in her stomach. "You're—you're sewing that poor beast's eyelids closed," she chattered.

"I shore am," Abel said and resumed his task. "Didn't you hear me say this steer spooked away from the bedground twice after he had been popped from the brush? This time I aim to see thet he stays in the brush an' heads no'th when I do."

"You're blinding him!" Lisa gasped.

"Only 'til this thread rots, which will be in a week or less," Abel said.

"How awful!" Lisa moaned.

"If it gravels you, ma'am, go back to the wagon an' stay out o' men's affairs."

Lisa turned and raced to the wagon, but not to hide her eyes. She snatched the whip from the socket and came storming back.

Abel looked at Micah and said, "As if I didn't have enough misery!"

"Turn that poor creature loose this instant," Lisa demanded, brandishing the whip.

Abel got to his feet. Lisa swung the whip, but an instant too late, for he had moved inside its arc. He plucked it from her hand and tossed it away. "I ought to tan your bottom for you," he said angrily.

"You're—you're vulgar!" Lisa blazed. "There's no decency in you."

"Not much, I reckon," he agreed calmly. "Runnin' cattle in the *brasada* ain't the sort o' thing calculated to make a dude out of a man."

He turned to the steer and poised the needle again.

"It's cruel!" she cried. "Unnecessary!"

"Tell me a better way to keep this jaybill with the herd," he demanded as he began plying the needle.

"That poor creature will die! It will starve!"

"Starve? A Longhorn?" Abel Barbee laughed rather sourly. "Why, ma'am, he'd rustle a livin' in hell. I'm doin' him a favor. He'll git fat an' sassy. Won't have ary a chance to run off the taller. Time he kin see to git ringy ag'in, he'll be fifty pounds heavier."

Abel Barbee added, "An' a hundred miles on his way no'th, I hope."

He worked fast as he talked, and the task was done before Lisa could think of further protest. He arose and carefully stored the needle and thread back in its packet—for future similiar use, Lisa realized. That thought again brought on the nausea.

Abel noticed her wan color. "Better git out o' sight, ma'am," he said. "If a little thing like that'll cold-chill you, then you'll jest naturally give up your insides at what I'm goin' to do to this whickerbill next."

"What do you mean?" Lisa asked faintly.

He walked to the fire, tested the handle of the length of iron and wrapped his neckerchief around it as a pad. He moved to the steer and pressed down the hot curved end of the iron, forming an insignia. The steer bawled mournfully. The odor of seared hide and burned hair assailed Lisa.

That did it. She raced into hiding beyond the wagon and was grateful for its shield. For, just as Abel Barbee had predicted, she was extremely nauseated.

CHAPTER *2*

Lisa recovered quickly and climbed shakily into the wagon. She chanced a glance. Abel Barbee was cooling the branding iron by scuffing it through loose earth. Micah had trod on the embers of the fire and was kicking dust over the spot.

The steer lurched to its feet, its dignity ruffled. It was tied to a tree by a short rope and its legs were hobbled. It seemed puzzled by its inability to open its eyes. It philosophically accepted the situation. To Lisa's annoyance, it even lowered its head and began munching at a tuft of grass.

Micah Jones climbed into the wagon and picked up the reins. "I'll join roundup in the morning, Abel," he said. "Sober. You can count on it."

Abel nodded. "I'll be obliged." He addressed Lisa, "Sorry you got bilious, ma'am."

Lisa ignored him. He persisted. "I take it they don't lid-sew cattle critters up no'th?"

"Good day, Mr. Barbee," she said frostily.

Micah started to release the impatient team, but pulled the animals to a halt again. A horseman had appeared on the trail, coming from the direction of San Ysidro. The rider lifted a shout, "Hold on a minute."

Abel Barbee rolled and lighted a brown-paper cigarette and stood drawing on it as the arrival rode up. "Afternoon, Kemp," he said. Lisa noted that his tone was carefully neutral.

"Hello, Abel," the man said. He was powerfully framed, with strong features. He had roan-colored sideburns and hair, and his eyes, which were set beneath strong brows, were of that same hue. He was a cattleman, by appearance, and his garb and the rigging on his horse were a cut or two above average in neatness and quality.

He removed his hat and looked at Lisa. "Good afternoon, ma'am. And you, Micah."

Micah made the introduction. "This is Kemp Travis," he informed Lisa. "He owns a ranch just east of here. Kemp, this is Miss Elizabeth Randolph."

"A pleasure, Miss Randolph," Travis said. "You must be the

young lady who arrived by stage today." He laughed and
added, "An event like that isn't likely to be passed by without
comment in San Ysidro, you can be sure."

Lisa decided that she was the reason for his presence. She
surmised he had galloped out from San Ysidro to overtake
the livery rig and get a look at her. "How do you do, Mr.
Travis," she said.

Travis twisted around in the saddle and eyed the captive
steer. He shifted his horse so that he could thoroughly in-
spect the original brand and also the fresh mark Abel Barbee
had burned in the creature's hide. He rode closer and Lisa
saw that he was eyeing the animal's ears, one of which
seemed to be disfigured.

Abel Barbee continued to calmly smoke his cigarette during
this. "Everything proper, Kemp?" he inquired. "Brand? Ear-
mark? Road brand?"

"I smelled smoke," Travis said.

"You got a real sharp nose," Abel Barbee commented.

Travis smiled. Lisa noted that he had a holstered pistol
beneath the skirt of his coat. "It won't be long before it'll
be against the law to build a branding fire on open range,"
he said.

Abel Barbee nodded. "Thet'll help stop thievin'."

"Or pack a running iron in a saddle boot," Travis added.

"Thet's where I carry mine," Abel said.

"I was on my way to Monte Vista to see if I could talk
Hester into pounding some sense into your head," Travis
said.

"Thet'd take some doin'," Abel replied. "I got a head like
a rock."

There had been no outward change in the tone of their
voices. Yet there had been a change. Lisa felt a small prickly
sensation move upward along her spine. She glanced at Micah
Jones for reassurance. Micah had been smiling. The rigid
form of the smile was still pasted on his lips, but it was a
sickly thing. His skin was the color of putty. With a shock
of apprehension she realized that she and Micah were in the
presence of a dark and bitter antagonism between two unyielding opponents.

Travis spoke. "Abel, I'll raise my offer to five dollars and
two bits a head for up to two thousand head of prime
beeves, fours and up, delivered to me within a week."

Abel shrugged. "They might fetch ten at Abilene. Maybe
more. Market might rise by late summer."

"But it's more likely to fall," said Travis. "Trail herds
went begging last year up north. Some are still up there, eating leased grass and putting their owners deeper in debt.

Such as didn't die in some of those Kansas blizzards. Others were sold for their hides. There's no sign of things bettering themselves. Then what'll you do when you get there?"

"Keep goin'," Abel said. "Find range somewhere an' squat. This is more than a trail herd we're gatherin'. We're movin' everything—hooves to horns."

"What does Hester think about quitting Texas?" Travis demanded.

"She's sad," Abel admitted. "But when a man can't road-brand his own cattle without a neighbor come bustin' over the hill, bent on hangin' him as a rustler, like you just did, it's time to make a move of some kind."

"I'll make the price five dollars, four bits," Travis said. "That's final."

"If the market is so bad why are you so all-fired eager to buy?" Abel asked.

"The only way a man can make expenses is to operate big right now," Travis declared. "I'm trying to shape up two drives. Maybe three. If I can come out two bits a head in the clear up there, it's better than sitting on my hands all season down here. Even a dime a head will keep me in coffee and cigars next winter."

"Sounds reasonable when you look at it your way," Abel remarked. "Lookin' at it my way I ain't interested in keepin' you in cigars an' coffee, Kemp."

Travis's voice sharpened a trifle. "You never give an inch, do you, Abel? I hope you and I never have any real trouble."

"That's a nice Christian-like hope," Abel agreed.

Travis turned to Lisa. "If there is any way I can help you, Miss Randolph, I'm at your service."

"Thank you," Lisa said.

He awaited further explanation, but when she offered none he broke the awkward moment by lifting his hat and turning to ride away. "I hope that we will meet again, soon," he said. He went jogging away in the direction from which he had come.

Micah Jones released the team, and the wagon lurched into fast motion. Micah drew a long breath as they went bounding away over the chuckholes. "That," he said, "was like sitting too close to a red-hot stove."

"Those two men didn't seem to care much for each other," Lisa observed.

"No," Micah said. "No, they don't."

Lisa looked back. Abel was walking toward his horse. The last view she had of him was of him lashing his rolled leather brush coat back of the cantle.

Abel concluded this task. He finished the cigarette and

ground the stub beneath his heel. He mounted and sat a moment gazing toward the empty trail where the spring wagon had rounded out of sight.

He glared accusingly at the captive steer. He started to dismount but decided against it. He rode a few paces, pulled up and fought it out with himself for a moment. At last he leaped from the saddle and walked to the animal. He snubbed its head tight against the mesquite tree. He drew a sharp knife and removed the stitches he had so recently placed. The steer, when he loosened the snubbing rope, snorted and tried to gore him.

Abel evaded that effort and stepped back into the saddle. "Damnation to you!" he addressed the steer fervently. "An' to all cattle."

He added, as he rode away, "And to all high-nosed females who look at a man like he wasn't fit to be seen."

CHAPTER 3

Lisa sat rigid and uncompromising in the spring wagon as she rode onward. The rank tang of burned hide seemed to cling to her. She shuddered. Everything about this land, she told herself, was harsh and elemental.

After a time she chanced a glance back. The scene of her encounter with Abel Barbee was lost among the brush and ridges. Off to the south she caught a brief glimpse of two horsemen. One was Kemp Travis.

Her thoughts kept swinging back to Abel Barbee. A small anger burned within her. She felt that, in his eyes, she had made a fool of herself. And she had to confess that he had considerable justification. She could not imagine what had come over her to impel her to try to use a buggy whip on him. Nothing like that had ever happened to her in her whole life.

"What will become of that poor creature?" she asked Micah.

"Become? You mean Abel?"

"Of course not! It's that dumb beast I'm concerned about. That cow."

Micah stared. "Why, bless you, Miss, in a week's time that steer will be raising hell—I mean, Cain—just like he was before. Abel will send out some gimpy old *cabestro* this afternoon and yoke 'em together."

"*Cabestro?*"

"That's Mex for a tame ox that leads others," Micah explained. "The ox will take that ringy cuss back to the holdout where he'll be glad to stay until he can see again."

Lisa didn't know what was meant by a holdout, and did not ask. "How cruel can a man be for profit?" she demanded.

Micah sobered. "Profit's been mighty hard to come by these last couple of years. Abel does only what has to be done. Bar B hopes for better luck in new country."

He saw the question forming and anticipated it. "Bar B is the main Barbee brand. Didn't you see it on that steer? And right ahead is Monte Vista where the Barbees live."

They had emerged onto a viewpoint which overlooked a wide sweep of lower country. This also was clothed with

14

brush. There were many sizable clearings. The yellow slash of a river bed wound across the flats. Far in the distance, low folded hills crouched on the horizon. There was no end to this thorned land—no beginning.

"This," said Micah, "is the heart of the San Ysidro cattle country. That stream you see is the San Ysidro River."

Close at hand, the buildings of a ranch headquarters were scattered among mesquite trees. Corrals stood in the open sun beyond the structures. Westward, in one of the clearings, Lisa made out the dark blotch of a herd of cattle held loosely on grazing. She saw two horsemen emerge from the brush into the clearing, rushing half a dozen cattle ahead of them. These were thrown in with the main herd.

"That's the Bar B holdout," Micah said. "They're well along toward getting shaped up for the trail, by the looks."

The wagon bounced down a grade, crossed the shallow stream and rolled into the ranch yard. A low, hip-roofed building that evidently served as a bunkhouse was constructed of split posts, set on end, and had a slab roof. Water in a foot-wide ditch cut across the yard and greened a pasture beyond.

A young, good-looking rider with tawny hair was shoeing a horse at a dirt-roofed work shed. Micah waved an arm in greeting. "Paul Drexel," he informed Lisa. "Rode for the Barbees since he was a boy. He's like one of the family. Most of the gals in the San Ysidro get giddy when Paul turns that smile of his loose."

Micah halted the rig before the main house. It stood low and solid, the doorsills almost at ground level. Lisa saw that it consisted of two buildings, connected by the roof, with a ten-foot walkway between.

The structures were made of the mud bricks, plastered and whitewashed. Judging from the depths of the window casings, the walls were up to two feet thick. The roof, supported by heavy posts, was extended to cover a gallery which ran the length of the two sections.

"Tom Barbee built the place to last," Micah observed. "Maybe it's just as well he doesn't know Bar B is about finished."

Lisa gazed, puzzled, at an object embedded in the heavily-timbered main door. It appeared to be a metal spearhead from which protruded a broken, foot-long wooden shaft.

Micah spoke in a matter-of-fact tone. "Comanche war lance. The Barbees left it there as a reminder."

"Reminder of what?" Lisa asked.

"The Comanches held the south house for more than a day, the Barbees the other. That was twelve years ago, come this summer. It was lucky Tom Barbee had the forethought to put up separate buildings, with the dogtrot between. That same bunch of Indians wiped out Paul Drexel's mother and father on their way here. Tom Barbee went under in the fight at this place. Hester killed the one who got Tom."

Lisa was startled. "Hester? The woman we're going to meet? She shot an Indian?"

"Her muzzle loader was empty," said Micah. "She used a pitchfork."

Lisa felt nausea threaten her once more.

Two women were busy over washtubs in the dogtrot. Beyond them, a washing flapped on a clothesline. One of the occupied pair was a young Mexican woman who wore a red petticoat and a thin cotton blouse and was barefoot.

The other was small, plump and energetic. Her graying hair was tightly pinned in a plaited coil on top of her head. She wore a linsey dress and a gingham apron, both of which despite the task that occupied her, showed a starched tidiness.

Only now did she become aware that visitors had arrived. With amazing vigor, she snatched up a rifle that had been placed handy. She paused with the weapon half-raised, the hammer back. "Micah!" she exclaimed. "You ought to know better'n to moccasin up on a person like that."

"I didn't expect you'd be that jumpy, Hester," Micah said. "After all, nobody's seen a hostile in the San Ysidro in a couple of years. It's time you settled down a little."

He alighted from the wagon. "This young lady is Miss Elizabeth Randolph, from Chicago, Illinois. Miss Randolph, meet Mrs. Hester Barbee, who can cook as good as she can shoot."

Hester Barbee dried her hands, removed her apron, hanging it on a wall peg, and came walking into the sunlight. Lisa noticed that the apron was made of the same blue and white check material as the shirt Abel Barbee had worn. Among the washing on the line was a second apron of the same cloth.

Hester Barbee had fine dark eyes. Understanding eyes. They were suspiciously bright at the moment. Lisa, puzzled, suspected that tears had been there at the time of their arrival.

"From Chicago, Illinois!" Hester Barbee exclaimed. "That's a faraway place. A scarey piece for a girl to travel."

She offered a hand. Lisa remembered that this hand had driven a pitchfork into a human body. She wanted to refuse, but lacked the courage. She found Hester's clasp gentle and assuring.

Micah helped her from the wagon and Hester led her into

the house. Coolness touched her. These walls had been built to ward off heat and cold as well as raiding Indians.

"This was our original house," Hester said. "One room. We added the others after the boys started to grow up."

The room evidently served for all occasions, formal or otherwise. A much-used spinning wheel stood in a corner, along with weaving equipment. The furniture was home-made, the settees and chairs slung with leather and rawhide.

The plank floor was bare, the furniture pushed back. Trunks and boxes and barrels stood along a wall, ready to receive household belongings.

"We're movin'," Hester said. "We can't take everything with us, of course. It's been a trial, selectin'."

There were depths to that statement that explained the tears she had been shedding in secret.

A picture in a carved frame, which stood ready for packing, caught Lisa's attention. It was a crayon portrait of a man and two boys. Done by an untrained hand, it showed an obvious talent, nevertheless.

"I made that of Tom an' the two boys the Christmas before he was taken away from us," Hester sighed. "I always liked to draw. Tom was a handsome one, now wasn't he? That's Matthew, my youngest, on the left. He's grown up to look just like his Pa. He was only ten then. Matthew's our dreamy one. He's always huntin' for a rainbow, whether it's in sunshine or storm. Some day he'll find it. The other one, lookin' so straight an' determined at us, is Abel, the oldest."

"Yes," Lisa said. "I recognize him by his eyes. I met Abel on the road today. His eyes haven't changed."

Hester's voice softened. "Abel's had the hard chores put on his shoulders. An' he had such other great plans. There was two others in between him an' Matthew. Twins. Frank an' William. We lost them when they was only six. The fever."

Hester shook off these memories and studied Lisa. "My! You're a tired girl, Elizabeth Randolph. An' lonely an' homesick. Wishin' you wasn't here, an' hopin' nobody finds out how panicky you are inside."

Lisa tried to speak and failed. Hester had looked right through her pride and had left her disarmed.

"Fetch some drinkin' water, Chepita!" Hester commanded. "Pronto!"

The Mexican girl hurried to obey and returned with an *olla* and a cup. Lisa sipped cool water. Micah Jones stood in the doorway, uncertain as to whether he wanted any part of this. Paul Drexel came walking to the gallery and gazed over Micah's shoulder, eyeing Lisa admiringly.

Hester patted Lisa's hand. "Blast my loose tongue! I didn't aim to unsettle you, young lady."

Lisa steadied, nettled at displaying weakness. This was the mothering hen, of whom she had made up her mind to be independent, and already she had placed herself at a disadvantage. "I'm all right now," she said. "Thank you."

She took a deeper breath and plunged in. "I came here to see a gentleman named Frank O'Hara."

"Frank O'Hara? Why, yes! O'Hara House is only a little piece west. Not much more'n half an hour's ride."

Like all the others, Hester did not ask the obvious question. Lisa, wanting to get this over with, answered it anyway. "I came here with the expectation of being married to Mr. O'Hara."

Hester Barbee stared at her, dumbfounded. Micah Jones and Paul Drexel backed hastily out of sight, and Lisa heard their footsteps receding across the yard.

Hester pushed Chepita toward the door. "Go back to the washin'," she commanded. "An' if I ketch you eavesdroppin' I'll lift your skelp."

She closed the door. "She'll listen. That's as certain as the sun settin'. If there's anythin' you don't want repeated, Elizabeth, don't say it."

"I have nothing to hide," Lisa said.

"Did I hear you right? About you aimin' to marry Frank O'Hara?"

"I said that was my expectation."

Hester sank down on a chair. "My land! Do you really mean that?"

Lisa had the breathless sensation of wading into icy water. "Is there any reason why I should not mean it?"

Hester gave her a new and very critical inspection. "Well, I wouldn't figure you two as havin' much in common."

Lisa arose. "Thank you for helping me, Mrs. Barbee. You say Mr. O'Hara's ranch is only a short distance . . . ?"

Hester interrupted her. "Where did you meet Frank?"

Lisa hesitated a moment. "In Chicago."

"Chicago? Why, Frank O'Hara never was in . . ." Hester paused, thinking, then resumed. "Come to remember it, he *was* there once. But that was three, four years ago."

"Four," Lisa said. "Four years this summer."

Hester peered at her. "So that's when you met him? But as I remember it, he wasn't there more'n a few days. He went there for a fling at high livin' after he sold a herd of cattle in Missouri. Frank took one of the first drives up north from the San Ysidro."

Lisa said nothing. Once more Hester's voice softened. "Maybe I'm beginnin' to see. You only laid eyes on him that once. Why, you couldn't been much more'n a child."

"I was old enough," Lisa said. "Nineteen."

She opened her reticule and brought from it a packet of letters. Among them was a tintype picture which she handed to Hester. "That's the way I remember Mr. O'Hara," she said. "My father brought him to our house for supper. My father was a broker, dealing in cotton. Mr. O'Hara was interested in investing the money he had made in the cattle sale."

"An' lost every cent when both cotton an' cattle went smash," Hester commented. She studied the picture. It was of a man of perhaps thirty, impeccably garbed from wing collar to elktooth watch charm. Frank O'Hara had the sensitively-cut features of blue-blooded ancestry, but there was self-indulgence in his handsome eyes and straight mouth.

Hester sighed. "He was a fine-lookin' one, wasn't he?"

"Do you mean that he has changed?" Lisa asked slowly.

Hester shrugged. "I'd say that this picture was taken in Chicago at the time you met him. Frank's the kind that can't stand adversity. You ain't the first picture bride what's found that things ain't like they was painted."

"Picture bride?"

"Not that it's any disgrace to be one. Fact is, I was a picture bride myself. Even more of a one than you. At least you had seen your man once. I never laid eyes on Tom Barbee 'til I got off the steamboat at St. Louis an' he was standin' there with a drawin' of me in his hand that I'd made of myself. Let me tell you that I had give myself a few little twinkles an' dimples that I didn't rightly have. But Tom Barbee wasn't Frank O'Hara."

Lisa fought against outward display of emotion. Inwardly, she was in complete chaos.

"I came from Ohio," Hester went on. "I worked in a woolen mill when I was a girl. Tom found my name in a sweater that he'd bought in Missouri, where he was tryin' to make a go of it at farmin'. He wrote a letter to me. That started it. That was almost thirty years ago. A few years after we was married, Tom decided we might do better in Texas. We finally came into the San Ysidro after the country got settled a little. I got a fine man, but it's my guess you could have had your pick of better'n Frank O'Hara. You 'pear to me to be one that was born with a satin pillow to lay your head on."

Lisa was silent. It seemed so pointless to explain to Hester how the satin pillow had been lost. Her father going to his grave penniless. Her mother following him a few months afterwards.

Trained only in the social graces, there had been few ways to earn a living of decency. She had worked as the nurse-maid of condescending friends who had made it plain that they felt they were extending charity.

That was why she had at last responded to the letters from the handsome cattleman, written to her regularly ever since the night he had proposed marriage, only a few hours after they had met.

At that time Frank O'Hara had been drinking the heady wine of success. He had been boisterously sure of himself and of his future. He had told her of his thousands of cattle and of O'Hara House, his mansion in Texas. He had frightened her with his impetuous, demanding courtship. She had fended him off, but she had never forgotten him. There had been in him an independence of thought and spirit, and a scorn of stuffy protocol. What he had come to represent to her was freedom—escape from the petty tyrannies and humiliations she was enduring.

Her first letters to him had been couched in the most decorous terms, but their real purpose had been obvious. These communications had extended over many months, for it had been a frightening decision for her to make.

Now she was here in a land whose loneliness shriveled her thoughts, among people who carried with them in their demeanor that same bold self-sufficiency that she had seen in Frank O'Hara. It was stamped on this small, gray-haired woman, Hester Barbee. It had been quietly there even in the calmness of Micah Jones' tolerant eyes. Above all, it had been sharp and challenging in Abel Barbee.

"What has happened to Mr. O'Hara?" she asked. "How has he changed?"

She waited, but came to accept the fact that Hester would never answer that question. Hester had gone as far as she considered proper into another person's affairs.

"Will I find Mr. O'Hara at his home?" she asked desperately.

"You better go back to town an' ketch the stage back to where you came from," Hester advised.

Lisa looked at her levelly. "I will see him, of course. He and I will decide this between us."

"What if things ain't like the way he painted 'em?"

"I'll cross that bridge when I come to it," Lisa said.

"Speakin' of bridges, it's my guess you've burned yours

behind you, Elizabeth. It ain't easy for a girl to turn back, once she's gone as far as you have. I know."

"That remains to be seen also," Lisa declared.

"Just what do you expect of Frank?" Hester asked.

Lisa considered that for a moment. "A home. Peace of mind. Faithfulness."

"An' what will you give him?"

Lisa answered that steadfastly. "My whole life. My loyalty. My fidelity."

"What you really want is the gold spoon again, Elizabeth."

Lisa did not attempt to evade. "Perhaps. I want security, at least. Integrity."

"Easy, soft livin'," Hester said harshly. "Well, you'll not find it here—not in cattle country. An' not with Frank O'Hara, above all."

Lisa moved toward the door. "I'm afraid you were right about the burned bridges and wanting the gold spoon, Mrs. Barbee," she said exhaustedly. "There will be no such thing as love involved in this marriage—if there is a marriage. That would have to come later. But, in any event, I would be a loyal wife."

Hester studied her for a moment. "You've got some spunk in you at that, Elizabeth Randolph," she said. "Wait! You need a woman at your side right now. I'll drive you to O'Hara House myself. I'll put a comb to my hair, an' change to somethin' more fit for visitin'."

CHAPTER 4

Lisa moved aimlessly around the room while she waited for Hester to return. She was shaken by what had been left unsaid, rather than anything Hester had told her. More than ever, she shrank from meeting Frank O'Hara.

She halted, distraught, before one of the deep-set windows. This east wall faced the back area. The washing flapped on the line just outside her range of vision. Two goats grazed on picket nearby. An ash hopper and a lye bucket, for use in making soft soap, stood at a distance.

A stone's throw away, trees and willows grew thickly along a small stream which had been dammed and which furnished the irrigation water for the ranch.

A man was walking toward the brush, following a narrow, beaten footpath. He evidently was one of the riding crew, by his garb. He looked back and saw Lisa's face at the window.

She turned away, retaining only an indifferent memory of brawn and height and heavy, sun-swart features. She resumed her restless pacing of the room.

It was a quarter of an hour before Hester returned, giving her hair a final preening before donning a bonnet, and issuing instructions to Chepita.

Lisa moved with her to the spring wagon. Micah Jones appeared at the door of the bunkhouse, but retreated thankfully when Hester called to him that she was taking over.

Paul Drexel came hurrying to assist Lisa into the vehicle. "It's my pleasure, Miss," he said. He was a very engaging person.

Hester handled the reins. They drove along the trail westward for some two miles and this brought them within closer view of the cattle in the clearing. The size of the herd at close range impressed Lisa. There were hundreds of the long-horned animals.

"They're poppin' the last of 'em out of the brush," Hester said, and once again there was a sigh in her voice. "We'll be leavin' soon, tryin' for a new start in new country. We fought Comanches an' the Lipans, an' even a bunch of Apaches who come this far down. Now we got to pull stakes an' likely will have to fight to put 'em down some-where else."

She was silent after that. The clearing fell behind and the trail carried them through swales among the brush-clumped hills. The faint, far thud of a gunshot echoed. Hester halted the team and listened for a time, but no further sound came.

A scatter of structures came into view. O'Hara House stood on a knoll. Against the background of brushy hills, it had an unreal, castle-like aspect. It seemed to be truly a mansion, built in the wealthy plantation style, with Doric columns rising to support galleries and the classic roof. Lesser buildings of posts and unpainted frame stood on lower ground.

The wagon carried them closer. Lisa sank back in the seat, a new hopelessness upon her.

The grandeur of O'Hara House had been an illusion. Its fine front was little more than a shell. Back of it, O'Hara House consisted of a squatty, low, sod-roofed structure.

The dilapidation of the mansion-that-might-have-been came into focus, little by little. Peeling paint and broken, sagging shutters. If there ever had been pane glass in the sashes, it had long ago vanished. Decay and neglect.

Lisa turned to Hester horrified. Hester spoke, sorrow in her voice. "The O'Haras came here from Georgia long before the war. They brought slaves an' had big plans. They aimed to get rich in cattle. They threw away what money they had. They found that buildin' a mansion in a wilderness was too much for them. Most of the slaves run away into Mexico. Only the front rooms of the mansion was ever finished. But they was just beautiful. They used to give such grand parties. I mind the time Sam Houston led the grand march at one. Now look at it. I feel like cryin'."

"He's—he's there?" Lisa asked shakily. "In this—this ghost house? Mr. O'Hara?"

"There's smoke from the kitchen. Frank has to do even his own cookin' these days. I reckon it's him that's home. Least-ways, he ought to be. Abel had to handle him a little rough yesterday. Frank likely don't feel up to stirrin' around much."

"Rough?" Lisa echoed. "What do you mean?"

Hester answered reluctantly. "You might as well know. Frank an' Abel had a ruckus in town. Frank wasn't himself. He tried to draw a gun on Abel."

"A gun?"

"Abel, so I was told, took it away from him before any real harm was done. But he had to knock Frank out with his fist to do it."

Lisa was horrified. "Mr. O'Hara was hurt?"

Hester smiled wanly. "Not bad. Only his pride. He'd been drinkin'. Abel had to do it or get shot. Men act mighty violent in these parts sometimes. It's a thing you got to learn to expect. There's been hard times, an' cattle not worth the salt they eat. Nerves have got on edge. Neighbors don't trust neighbors. Frank an' Abel have been mighty good friends. Now they've fought, an' fought bitter."

"I should not have come to this—this awful country!" Lisa burst out.

Hester made no comment. She halted the rig before wide stone steps which mounted to a crumbling flagstone walk leading to the main doors of O'Hara House. The surroundings had once been cleared for a huge lawn that had never been planted. Mesquite and other thorned growth had returned and were well on its way toward enfolding the place.

Hester sat waiting. Lisa realized that the decision was all her own. She looked at the looming house. One of the double doors stood ajar. At a broken window, a tattered, stained lace curtain swayed slightly in the breeze. The smoke that drifted above the roof from the rear seemed heavier in volume. Lisa decided that the stove was being stoked. However, an utter silence lay over the place.

She braced herself and alighted. She stood a moment, for every step required a driving effort of her will. She began moving up the weed-lined walk toward that empty door.

She now saw the first sign of other life. A horseman was visible some distance south of the ranch. He was amid the brush. The foliage hid even his horse. Only his upper body was in view. He seemed to be sitting there, gazing in the direction of O'Hara House. He apparently sighted Lisa. He abruptly rode away, disappearing into the thickets.

The only identifiable item that Lisa marked at that distance was the blue and white pattern of his shirt. Abel Barbee.

The creak of wheels arose. Hester had swung the rig and was driving away. Lisa started to protest, but Hester called, "I'll be back in an hour or so. I'll drive to the holdin' ground an' pass the time of day with the boys."

Lisa realized that it was best that she and Frank O'Hara work this out alone. She moved mechanically toward the house. Hester and the wagon faded out of sight into the hills eastward.

Lisa tapped on the door. The varnish that had once glistened on its panels was dissolved into scabrous ridges. The catch was broken.

No answer came. The only sound was the soft stirring of the window curtain. The door creaked a few inches farther open. She could see into the main room. Its condition matched the outward appearance of O'Hara House. Disorder and confusion. Furniture broken, grimy and neglected; saddles and other gear were tossed on sofas and chairs; empty whiskey jugs and bottles lay scattered about. Some had been smashed against the walls.

She called out in a small voice, "Mr. O'Hara?"

There was only the swishing of the curtain. She was drawn onward by the heart-swelling, intuitive impression that someone was present.

She walked through the big room and into the low-roofed log structure at the rear. The O'Haras had used this as their living quarters.

A man lay sprawled, face down, on the floor, an arm folded to support his head as though he were asleep.

He was not asleep. A dark stain of blood had spread beneath his body. Lisa realized that this was Frank O'Hara. He was not the man she remembered. Like the house, he had aged and fallen toward ruin. He was unshaven, gaunt, dissipated.

He was still alive. His head moved and his eyes were turned toward her. Something warm and wondering came into them. "Elizabeth!" he said in a fading voice. "You—you did come here? You kept your word. I should not have done this to a gentlewoman. Forgive . . ."

He stopped talking. He was still looking at her, vast yearning in his eyes. It was as though he was gazing at all of the great things of life that he had wanted.

She knew in the next moment that he was no longer seeing her, or seeing anything. She knelt beside him and stroked back his hair. "I'm sorry," she murmured. "So dreadfully sorry, Frank O'Hara."

She now saw the source of the blood on the floor. Frank O'Hara had been shot in the back. She remembered the distant report of a gun that she and Hester had heard.

She arose, trembling. She became aware of the strong tang of smoke. It came from a door to her left. She ran to the opening. It led into a kitchen. Flames had climbed a log wall and were enveloping the beams of the roof. The cooking had been done in a wide fireplace, equipped with hooks and swing arms. A supply of fuel stood nearby on the floor and was burning furiously. This was the source of the destruction that was setting in.

A cedar water pail stood on a bench. Lisa hurled its meager contents. The water was absorbed with no result. The fire began to roar.

Lisa retreated to Frank O'Hara's body. She lifted his weight by the shoulders and backed, dragging him, through the main

room and across the entry and down the walk to a safe
distance. The scuffing sounds of his boot heels, grating on the
flagstones, sickened her.

Flame appeared among the smoke above the classic front
of O'Hara House. Terror gripped Lisa. She removed her dust
coat and covered Frank O'Hara's body. Gathering her skirts
she began running away from the burning effigy of a mansion.
She ran down the wagon trail in the direction Hester had
driven. She burst into screaming.

She fell, arose and ran ahead, struggling against the pitiless
distances of this lonely land. Back of her, O'Hara House was
shrouded in flame. She looked back. Only the pillars were dis-
tinguishable, and these seemed distorted and leaning crazily.

She kept running. From a rise she sighted the Bar B herd
far away in the big meadow. A rider appeared from the brush
nearby and came up at a gallop. He alighted with lank agility.
That, along with the distinctive gingham shirt of blue and
white check that he wore, identified him.

She screamed again—shrilly. She fainted, folding up in the
dust at Abel Barbee's feet.

He said, "Lord a'mighty! Don't take on like that!"

He drew his pistol and fired three shots in the air. In the
distance riders with the herd had already sighted the fire and
were coming at a gallop.

Abel bent and lifted Lisa from the dust into his arms. He
looked down at her and murmured, "Ain't you the purty one,
though!"

Lisa revived. She looked up and recoiled from him. "Put me
down," she breathed.

"What happened?" he demanded.

As if he didn't know! She stared at him with fear. Other
riders arrived. To them she babbled, "It's Frank O'Hara! He's
dead. Murdered. He died looking at me. So sad! So sad!"

She kept repeating it. She couldn't quit talking. Abel shook
her. "Quit it!" he commanded.

He placed her on her feet, steadying her until he was certain she would not collapse again. Men rode away toward the
tower of fire that had been O'Hara House.

Events became somewhat confused for Lisa. Hester arrived
with the spring wagon and Lisa found herself being lifted
into the vehicle by Abel.

Afterward, she sat in the thick-walled stronghold at Monte
Vista. Chepita and Hester came with smelling salts and cold
compresses. These she pushed aside. All that had happened
was suddenly vividly clear in her mind.

Abel was standing in the background, leaning against the
frame of a doorway. His hands hung passively at his sides.

Even in this attitude she was aware of the suppressed energy within him, the restrained restlessness.

She gazed at the checked gingham shirt that he wore. An anger began to hammer at her. And revulsion. A darkening frown pinched at his lean features. She knew he had seen the accusation in her face. She turned away from him. There was no telling what steps he might take if he became sure that she had dangerous knowledge.

Another man was in the room. The resemblance to Abel told Lisa who he was. He could be no other than Matthew, the younger brother, whom Hester had described as the dreamy one.

In height the brothers were about equal. Physically, Abel had the advantage, being broader of shoulder. Matthew was slim, young, lithe and with fine dark eyes in which burned a quiet fire. His eyes were like Hester's. There was something of that same inner flame in Abel. But with a difference. Abel's gaze was demanding. He would tolerate no evasion or subterfuge. In Matthew, she sensed, was a forbearance of the frailty of human nature.

Like Abel, the younger brother's garb bore the dust of hard saddle work.

And, like Abel, he wore a shirt of the distinctive blue and white pattern!

Lisa sat staring incredulously from brother to brother as this last fact drove home. She saw the frown deepen in Abel, saw puzzlement in him as though he did not understand. Matthew, who stood with a boot on a chair, did not move or change expression as he endured her inspection.

Hester spoke in a murmur in Lisa's ear. "I made both of them shirts for my boys a few weeks ago. I bought ten yards of cloth at Al Halley's store in San Ysidro. Paid for it with two head of beef steers an' a bullhide to boot. He charged a dollar a yard, but I couldn't resist."

Their eyes met and clashed. Hester spoke again, in a casual, chatting tone. "Al had a whole bolt of that gingham in stock. It could be possible that other mothers or wives made shirts for their men from that same piece of cloth."

In Hester was a fierce, maternal protectiveness that amounted to a challenge. Lisa realized that Hester also must have seen that rider who had vanished into the brush, fleeing from the scene of the murder of Frank O'Hara.

This, then, was the answer of the Barbee clan to what was in her thoughts and to any accusation she might make.

She was sure that Matthew's garb was no matter of coincidence. Hester had seen to it that he had donned the checked shirt before appearing in her presence.

The rider she had glimpsed could, of course, have been either of the brothers. At that distance, she doubted if even Hester could have been sure which of her sons it might have been.

But in Lisa's memory was the echo of Hester's own words at the time they had gazed at the crayon drawing of Tom Barbee and his sons. . . . ". . . Abel's had the hard chores put on his shoulders. . . ."

Abel spoke. "Do you want to tell us all about it?"

"Yes," Lisa said. But there were reservations in her mind as she began to relate the finding of Frank O'Hara in the burning house. She did not tell Abel that she believed he was the guilty one. Nor did she mention the rider she had seen. She left it to Hester to place him on guard. She was certain Hester would do just that.

CHAPTER 5

Frank O'Hara's funeral was to be held the following afternoon. The burial was to be within sight of the ashes of O'Hara House in a plot of ground that held the graves of his parents and two brothers and other kinsmen.

"Frank was the last of his family," Micah Jones told Lisa. "The O'Hara men all went about the same way. Cards, whiskey, duels. The wives and mothers died early too, often of broken hearts, I'm afraid. Frank's father was killed in a pistol duel over some affront to his dignity. His eldest brother was shot in a row over a poker game. The other brother died in a fall while riding to hounds, trying to spear javelinas in the brush when he was dead drunk. And now there are no more O'Haras. No more like them. Bless their memory."

Lisa spent the night in San Ysidro, finding quarters with an elderly couple who managed the stagecoach station. Hester had offered the hospitality of Monte Vista but, when Lisa refused, did not insist.

Lisa had Micah drive her back to O'Hara House very early the next morning, so early in fact that they arrived shortly after sunup. She was surprised to find Abel and Matthew Barbee, along with Paul Drexel, had stood all-night vigil over Frank O'Hara's bier. The only ones.

The body lay beneath a sheet in a small house which evidently had been the home of some married foreman or clerk in the prosperous days of Triangle O, which, Lisa learned, was the brand the O'Haras had used. On the knoll, smoke rose thinly from the charred debris of the mansion.

The brothers wore dark town suits, white shirts and black string ties. Lisa again marked their similarity in appearance and knew the impossibility of naming either definitely as the one she had seen riding away from O'Hara House.

It was Paul Drexel who came hurrying to assist her from the wagon. He lifted her down, his hands gripping hard on her arms. He held her thus, far longer than was necessary, her toes barely touching the ground, gazing at her with a bold promise and a challenge in his blue eyes.

29

"You're a feather," he said. "No! A cloud. One of Matthew's golden clouds. With pretty red hair."

"I won't float away, I promise you," Lisa said. "Now if you'll just put me down."

He laughed. He held her a moment longer. He wore a natty dark saddle shirt, a pistol belt and breeches stuffed into threaded boots. He released her, letting his hands slide slowly down her arms. She swung away from him, color warming her. She saw that Abel Barbee was observing this, a cynicism in his dark eyes. That brought anger within her.

"Mr. Jones said they're going to hold an inquest," she said. "There's considerable straightening up to do."

"The bunkhouse is the only place big enough," he said. "It needs reddin' up, but Hester'll be along soon, an' other women. There's no call for you to soil your hands."

It was plain he did not believe that her efforts at housecleaning would amount to much. She left him and entered the small house where she stood beside Frank O'Hara's body for a time. He was handsome in death, almost as handsome as he had been the night they had met. But he was a stranger. She might have married him, but she doubted that now.

She had learned some things about Frank O'Hara from Jenny Calvert, the wife of the stage agent, during her overnight stay in town. And also about Abel Barbee.

The two men had been close friends, even though they appeared to have little in common, one the hard-drinking, aristocratic, irresponsible scapegrace, the other unschooled, dedicated to the rough profession of raising cattle.

"Just what caused 'em to fall out, nobody rightly knows," Jenny Calvert had said. "Frank was drinking. They talked for awhile, and then it started. Frank tried finally to pull a gun and Abel knocked him down and took the gun. All anybody heard Abel say was, 'You sot!' "

Jenny Calvert had added, "Some say it was because Frank went back on a promise to throw in with the Barbees and move north. But I say it was over a woman. Aren't we the root of all evil?"

Lisa had disappointed her by refusing to pursue the subject. She had known that every move she made, every word she spoke, would be discussed by the people of San Ysidro.

She turned away from the bier and went out softly, leaving Frank O'Hara alone.

Abel and the other men were awaiting her. She had brought a cotton housedress and a dust cap in a handbag, and she donned them in the privacy of the cookhouse. Searching in the cluttered room, she located a broom and scrub pail and brush, none of which apparently had been used in some time.

Thus armed, she marched into the bunkhouse. This, like the house, had originally been planned on a grand scale to quarter slaves. Only a portion had been completed. The unfinished end had been boarded off, and had stood that way for years. Even so, the remainder was sizable. It had suffered the same neglect as had the mansion. Yellowed pamphlets, broken dishes, whiskey jugs and cigarette stubs littered the floor. Lisa pitched in and the dust began to swirl.

Abel entered. She ignored him but was very much aware of his scrutiny. He finally sighed and pulled off his coat and necktie. "Seems like you could use a mite of help," he observed. "It ain't rightly in my line."

"No," she said. "It isn't."

He flushed a trifle at the way she had corrected his grammar. "Rough-handlin' cow brutes an' torturin' 'em with a runnin' a'rn an' a needle is more my caliber," he said. "Is thet what you're tryin' to say?"

"Apparently you don't restrict your rough-handling to cattle," she said.

"I reckon you mean my trouble with Frank O'Hara."

"I understand you struck him with your fist while he was under the influence of liquor. That was being very fair now, wasn't it?"

"Under the influence?" he snorted. "He was mean drunk."

He took the broom from her hands and began wielding it angrily. "I told him thet the next time I found him likkered, I'd whale the tar out'n him. I didn't aim to stand by an' let him make a fool out of himself."

"A fine way to preach," Lisa said. "Dragging his pride in the dust in a street brawl."

"It was his pride I was tryin' to lift out'n that dust," Abel declared. "Frank O'Hara, when he was sober an' sound, wasn't one a man could slam around. I'd have been in fer a hell of a fight, I reckon, if I could have got him mad enough to have sobered up and come to his right senses."

He picked up an empty stone whiskey jug and, in a rage, hurled it against a wall, shattering it. "An' now he's dead!" he burst out. "I wanted him to trail no'th with us. It'd have been the savin' of his soul."

Lisa gazed at the broken jug. "As if this place isn't littered enough," she protested weakly.

She would, she told herself, be only too thankful when she could leave this alien land and its violent-tempered, unpredictable inhabitants. She had already made arrangements to take the eastbound stage for San Antonio the following day. She would return to the drab but orderly existence of the past.

Paul Drexel and Matthew appeared, attracted by the crashing of the jug. They took a look at Abel's lowering countenance and seemed to understand.

Paul swept off his hat to Lisa. "At your service, Elizabeth," he said. "What do your friends call you? Beth? Betty?"

"Never mind thet," Abel spoke. "Help get this damned pigsty fixed up. You too, Matt."

More forcibly than before, Lisa was reminded that both Matthew and Paul Drexel had the advantage of formal educations which Abel lacked.

The four of them brought an appearance of tidiness to the place. Damaged chairs and benches were removed or made presentable. The litter on the floor was conquered.

Presently Hester Barbee arrived, along with Chepita. Other ranch women also appeared, and gave a hand at finishing the housecleaning. But Lisa had the satisfaction of knowing that the improvement was due mainly to her own efforts. She felt that Frank O'Hara would have preferred it that way.

There was approval in Abel Barbee's manner, but Hester said, disappointed, "There ain't much more thet we can do. You ought to have let me come with you in the first place, Elizabeth Randolph."

A flood of arrivals came pouring in. The inquest was called to order shortly before noon in the bunkhouse.

Lisa was the first witness and was asked to tell in detail the finding of Frank O'Hara dying. The room was crowded and stuffy. The number who had appeared was a revelation to Lisa. It came to her that they were here not so much to pay their respects to the memory of Frank O'Hara as to take a look at the female who had come here from the north to marry him.

There was a stir and a tense leaning forward when she related Frank O'Hara's words, "I should not have done this to a gentlewoman. . . ."

Lisa had believed that it wouldn't matter: that she was speaking of a stranger. She was wrong. She halted and suddenly had to fight tears until she could control her voice again.

"Did he say who killed him?" asked Clem Temple, the man in charge of the coroner's jury.

"No," Lisa said. "Perhaps there wasn't time. But it's my belief he did not know."

"When did the house catch fire?"

"It evidently was burning before I arrived. There was smoke, but we—Mrs. Barbee and I—took it for granted it came from the chimney."

"You say it seemed to have started among the fuel in the woodbox. Did you try to put it out?"

It came to Lisa that there was hostility in the question, and in the many faces that were staring at her. "Yes," she said slowly. "But it had gotten too much of a start."

"Is there anything else you want to say?" Temple asked.

"Yes," Lisa replied. "I saw someone leaving O'Hara House. At least he apparently had been there."

There was a startled stir. "Who . . . what . . . ?" Clem Temple asked, excited.

"I saw a rider disappearing into the thickets off to the south of the ranch," Lisa explained. "I saw him as I was moving up the walk to the front door. He was too far away to make out his identity positively but . . ."

Her glance passed swiftly over Abel Barbee who stood at the rear of the crowded room. ". . . but I am certain he was wearing a shirt of a blue and white pattern of some kind."

The majority of the onlookers appeared puzzled. A few seemed to know the significance of what she had said, for she saw their attention swing to the Barbees—and then swing hurriedly away.

Abel came walking down the room. He was glaring fiercely at her as though he wanted to pluck the truth right out of her. "Why didn't you tell us this before?" he demanded.

He was either a good actor and had been prepared for this, or Hester had withheld from him the knowledge of sighting that retreating rider. His surprise seemed genuine.

"Hold on, Abel!" Clem Temple protested. "I'm doing the questioning. Now, young lady, are you plumb positive you saw this person?"

There was skepticism in the man's voice. Lisa, shocked, realized he felt that she was lying. She looked at the staring faces. Suddenly she knew! They were of the opinion that she had murdered Frank O'Hara herself. That caused her to partly rise, gazing around in angry challenge.

"Anything wrong, lady?" Clem Temple asked.

"You believe me, don't you?" she demanded.

Neither Temple, nor any of the other four men on the panel, would meet her eyes. "Any reason we shouldn't?" Temple asked.

Lisa again inspected the onlookers. "I don't care what you think," she said grimly.

They excused her. She started to leave the room, but heard

them call Abel Barbee. She halted and found a seat in the background.

Abel didn't wait to be questioned. Nor did he bother to take the witness chair. He remained on his feet. "Here's what I know," he said. "I was headin' back to the herd to send out oxen to bring in a couple of *ladinos* I had staked out in the brush. I saw O'Hara House on fire. I came acrost Miss Randolph runnin' up the trail. She told me somethin' had happened to Frank. She keeled over."

"Got any idea who did it, Abel?" Temple asked hesitantly.

"If I did I wouldn't be wastin' time here," Abel said.

.There was wariness in Temple's tone. "You and Frank had a fight the day before yesterday."

Abel's voice was casual. "Yeah. An' yesterday, I was wearin' a shirt o' the kind Miss Randolph jest described. Blue an' white check."

From the rear of the room Matthew Barbee spoke clearly. "So was I."

Matthew added casually, "Miss Randolph can verify that."

Nobody said anything for a time. Or even moved. Clem Temple sighed, breaking the silence. "I reckon there's no harm in wearin' a checked shirt. That'll be all, Abel."

Abel walked down the room through that silence. He gave Lisa a brief look and she saw in him a deep and lingering question. It was as though she held for him the solution to a problem so elusive that it angered him.

Nobody else was gazing directly at him. *They're afraid of him,* Lisa thought. *Some believe I killed Frank O'Hara, others are sure it was he, but they haven't the courage to accuse him. They will accuse me.*

The verdict was returned swiftly and informally after a whispered conference among Temple and his panel. "Looks like Frank was shot by a person or persons unknown," Clem Temple announced. "Leastwise that's the way it stands right now, 'til more evidence turns up."

Lisa glanced around. Matthew stood near the door. He had a shoulder canted against the wall. He had removed his coat. The breath drove sharply back into Lisa. Matthew wore a brace of holstered six-shooters.

Hester also sat in the room among the crowd. She wore black taffeta and a black-veiled bonnet in respect to the dead. She was rigid of body, her lips tight. Lisa noted the pallor in her face—and the determination. As surely as though she could see the weapon, she knew that Hester also was armed. The Barbees had come here prepared to overawe or resist any attempt to arrest Abel or Matthew for Frank O'Hara's murder.

The gathering broke up. A rush began to escape from the confinement of the room. Micah Jones, who was taking seriously his duties as Lisa's escort, came to her side as she walked into the ranch yard.

Another man moved up. He was Kemp Travis, of the roan-colored sideburns. "Good afternoon, Miss Randolph," he said, removing his hat. "You remember me, I trust?"

"Of course, Mr. Travis. It was only yesterday that we met, wasn't it? That seems a long time ago."

Travis smiled. "Things have happened, or maybe were pushed into happening."

He gave Micah a look, and Micah found matters elsewhere that drew him out of earshot.

Hester had seated herself on a bench in the shade of a tree and was using a black lace fan. Matthew and Abel were near her. Paul Drexel stood in the background alone. Again Lisa was shocked. Paul Drexel also wore a brace of pistols in bullhide holsters. It was plain that he was ready to join in with the Barbees in anything that came up. Only Abel seemed to be unarmed.

Kemp Travis studied the Barbees with heavy deliberation. "A lot of people think Abel killed Frank," he said.

"And some believe I did it," Lisa remarked.

He eyed her quizzically. "I hardly expected you to say that. However, I like people who are frank."

"Which do you believe is the guilty one?" Lisa asked. "Mr. Abel Barbee or myself?"

Travis laughed softly. "The more I come to know you, the more you interest me." He drew a cigar from a case, asked her permission with an inquiring glance, clipped its end and lighted it. "What are your plans for the future, Elizabeth?"

"I'm taking the eastbound stage out of San Ysidro tomorrow. I will go back to Illinois, I imagine."

"And then . . . ?"

"Why, I'll . . ." Lisa's voice drifted off.

Travis's knowing smile appeared again. "Exactly. What then? You came here to escape from something. There's no returning. You know that."

Lisa stood silent. He was right. Hester Barbee had voiced the same thought. She could not go back.

"There's no need for it, anyway," Travis said. "I'm a bachelor. I own cattle and range—considerably more than any other man in the San Ysidro. Like the rest, I've not done too well financially lately. That's changing. I'll be back on my feet before another winter. In a few years I'll be rich. I need a wife. A lady. A lady with breeding, to run my household. A wife like you."

"You can't be serious!" Lisa exclaimed

"Deeply serious. I'm asking you to marry me."

Lisa frowned, touched by a sudden resentment. He saw this and laid a hand on her arm. "What's wrong with that? You came here to marry O'Hara, almost sight unseen. You thought you were marrying well. Now you have a real chance."

"Thank you," Lisa said.

He eyed her frowningly. "For what?"

"For letting me see myself as others see me. I'm not a lady, after all."

He laughed. "Marrying for money is hardly a sin."

"There's a little more to it than that," Lisa said.

She turned and walked away. He overtook her long enough to say, "You'll look at it my way after you think it over. You're a sensible person."

CHAPTER 6

Frank O'Hara lay in state until mid-afternoon. The coffin was placed on a black-draped ranch wagon, drawn by four plumed horses. The assembly followed the carriage on foot to the family burial plot. There a minister preached and prayed for an hour.

There was doleful wailing and sniffling among some of the women who attended, but Lisa saw that the purpose was to draw attention to the mourner, rather than any display of real affection for the man whose coffin was lowered into the earth.

Lisa did not weep, but in her was a deep pity for Frank O'Hara. And a realization of kinship. He had been lonely, driven by his need for understanding and companionship, just as she had been. Evidently, whatever his faults, only he had suffered from them. And surely he had not deserved to die in the manner in which his life had been taken.

She looked up and found Abel Barbee's gaze upon her. Once more she was aware how intensely he was studying her, asking himself a question. Was he trying to determine the extent of her knowledge of that person in the checked shirt? Or was there accusation in his mind?

She turned away the moment the final "amen" was uttered. Micah Jones had remained close at her side. She took his arm and guided him to the rented spring wagon where the team, unharnessed and tied to a tree, munched from nose-bags.

"I want to start back to San Ysidro at once," she said wearily.

Micah began hooking up the team, but before they were ready to leave, a man in a black frock coat came hurrying from the bunkhouse, followed by a string of ranch people.

"Miss Randolph!" the man exclaimed. "Wait! I'm about to read the will. We've been waiting for you."

"The will?" Lisa repeated.

"Frank O'Hara's will. I'm Samuel Miller, attorney at law. I drew up Frank's testament some two weeks ago, at his request."

37

Lisa was suddenly afraid. She started to ascend into the wagon, but Sam Miller halted her. "Wait, please! I'm sure this will interest you. I know the contents, of course."

He produced a document and read it, rattling off the legal terms dramatically. He looked up triumphantly. His face fell when he realized that Lisa had not been listening. "Don't you understand?" he exclaimed. "You're the sole heir to this place and all range rights and all Triangle O cattle. Frank O'Hara left you everything. Everything!"

Lisa took the paper from his hand. But it was not the legal document that interested her. To that instrument was pinned a smaller, hand-written letter on a woman's personal stationery.

Then Lisa wept for the murdered Frank O'Hara. The letter was hers. It was the last message she had written to him before setting out on her long journey to San Ysidro. It contained her decision to consider marriage.

Sam Miller was nodding. "It was your letter that decided him on making out the will in your favor. He told me all about you."

Lisa became aware of other faces around her, and of their hostility. A ranch woman in the background spoke raucously, "Well, she got what she came fer, after all. She's been given the O'Hara ranch—fer what it's worth."

"I don't want it!" Lisa exclaimed, her voice rising.

"You can refuse, of course," Sam Miller said dubiously. "There are no other heirs. The courts will take over."

"Then I do refuse, and——" Lisa began.

A man stepped to her side, halting her. "Don't do any decidin' yet." It was Abel Barbee. He drew her out of hearing range of the others.

"But I don't want it," Lisa said. "I can't possibly accept."

"Maybe you've got the wrong idea about the O'Hara ranch," Abel said. "The house is gone, but thet don't stop cows from droppin' calves or the brand from increasin'."

"What difference would that make? It's that——"

"I'm tryin' to tell you thet Triangle O cattle are worth some money. Not a lot, of course. But somethin', if you get 'em to no'thern market. Even a little's better'n nothin', ain't it, after the long ways you come to get it?"

Lisa slapped him then, hard. As hard as she could. She turned and raced to the spring wagon. Micah Jones was waiting alongside the vehicle, but he made no move to help her mount to the seat. He stood looking at her, a moody speculation in his bony face.

"There might be other reasons why you ought to go slow about refusing, Miss Randolph," he said.

"Reasons? I'm sure there could be none that would make me change my mind."

"Somebody," Micah said slowly, "must have had some purpose in mind in killing Frank O'Hara."

"What do you mean?"

"What's one big reason why people murder others? For profit of some kind. Money, usually."

Lisa quieted, gazing at him, waiting. He nodded, and went on, "There might be someone who wants to get his hands on Frank's cattle and range. Maybe they're worth more than people think."

"Who could this someone be?" Lisa asked. "Abel Barbee, perhaps?"

Micah frowned. "Abel has an interest," he conceded. "Frank had promised to throw in with the Barbees. Between them, they figured they could market enough beef steers, no matter what the price, to give them a start at buying range and breeder stock up north. As it stands, with just the Bar B going it alone, Abel would be operating on a mighty thin string."

"You're building up a very strong case against Abel Barbee," Lisa said. "You know that, don't you?"

"Maybe. But I could point at others."

"Who, for instance?" Lisa asked.

But Micah shook his head, refusing to answer.

"Why didn't Mr. O'Hara go through with his promise to the Barbees?" Lisa asked.

"I have a hunch you're the cause."

Lisa hadn't expected that. "I?"

"It looks like Frank changed his mind about leaving Texas when he found that he might be married," Micah explained. "And he got to drinking harder than ever."

"Why? The drinking, I mean?"

Micah shrugged. "Guilty conscience, most likely. He, let us say, misrepresented things to you, did he not? He was probably afraid to face you. That's the way with hard drinkers."

Lisa stood torn by doubt. She knew now that she was the woman Jenny Calvert had referred to as the cause of the fight between Abel Barbee and Frank O'Hara.

"What good would it possibly do if I were to accept Mr. O'Hara's property?" she asked.

"Maybe it'd help turn up the real reason why Frank was killed. At any rate, it would keep Triangle O in the hands of the person he wanted to have it. And out of the paws of any who wanted it so bad they'd commit murder to get it."

Lisa said wanly, "You make me feel that I'd be helping the guilty man by refusing to accept."

"It could be that way," Micah nodded. "Then there are other reasons. Frank lived high. He plunged when he gambled. He won his share, but lost a lot lately. He borrowed money from friends over the last few years. He was honest. He'd have paid off, if he'd lived. But he left some debts. I think he'd rest easier in his grave if someone he could trust would take over Triangle O and see that those who helped him got a fair shake out of the estate."

"You're leaving me no choice," Lisa said.

Hester was approaching, her manner dubious, as though she expected rebuff. "I do hope you make up your mind to stay in the San Ysidro country, Elizabeth," she said.

"I'm going to do that," Lisa said, reaching her decision suddenly. "At least until the man who shot Mr. O'Hara is found."

Again the fierce maternal challenge flared in Hester. "I'd be pleased if you'd live at Monte Vista 'til you get settled," she said. "There's a nice room we can fix up."

"But you are leaving Monte Vista?"

"It'll be another week or so, Abel tells me. You'll be welcome to make your home there as long as you care to stay. We're not sellin' the place just yet. Couldn't, even if we wanted to, I reckon, unless we gave it away for almost nothin'. After we've found a place to settle up north, we'll decide what to do." Hester added wistfully, "Maybe we'll come back. Maybe we won't like it up there." She tried to smile. It was a dismal failure. "It's real hard, leavin' a place that you built from the roots. The boys' handprints are in some of the 'dobe with which we made the first house. Matthew was only a baby."

"I'll be glad to accept your offer," Lisa said. She again had come to an abrupt decision. Breaking bread under the same roof with Abel Barbee had been the last thing she had had in mind a moment earlier. But it had occurred to her that this might give her an opportunity to study the brothers and decide positively which was the one she had seen leaving O'Hara House. It must certainly have been Abel. It was difficult to associate Matthew with a matter of such violence. But she must make sure.

Hester, who was watching her closely, said, "I'm real pleased that you decided it that way. We want to get to know you better, Elizabeth. An' we want you to know us Barbees better, too."

Again they gazed at each other, the issue clearly defined between them. Hester knew why Lisa was coming to Monte Vista, and she meant to protect her sons with every weapon she possessed.

CHAPTER 7

Lisa was spared the ordeal of facing Abel and Matthew at their own table on this first night at Monte Vista. Just as the meal was being served by Chepita and Hester, a rider came galloping into the yard, shouting for Abel.

"Damnation to hell!" Abel exclaimed. "I ain't ever et a peaceful meal in my life. Come on!"

He and Matthew ran out of the house. They were joined by other men from the bunkhouse. Lisa heard them saddle up and go riding away into the darkness.

Hester stood in the door for a time, listening. "Trouble with the cattle," she finally sighed. "They had a run, an' the boys on night guard couldn't hold 'em. Some of 'em busted into the shinnery, I reckon. But it's my guess the main bunch is settin' tight. If all of 'em had spooked, you'd hear 'em clean down here."

She realized that Lisa didn't understand and tried to make it clearer. "Cattle air the cussedest pests. They'd try the patience of Job. They run when nothin's happened. They stand still when they ought to run."

Lisa peered from the window into the blackness through which the men were riding. The rushing sound of hooves faded, and no other information came back. She shivered.

She and Hester ate alone. But Hester's mind was not on what was before them. "Seems like I'm everlastin'ly waitin' 'til the cattle are taken care of," she said. In that protest was the lament of years of lonely meals and of long nights of worrying about menfolk who had gone galloping away into other such blacknesses.

Afterwards, Lisa sat in the bedroom that Hester and Chepita had prepared for her. Candles in heavy brass holders burned on the dressing stand. The bed was made of hand-hewn walnut. There was a highboy, along with a chair and a washstand. A niche in the whitewashed wall contained a Spanish-made Station of the Cross, done in colored plaster. A prayer bench stood beneath it.

Monte Vista seemed to be settling down for the night. She opened her luggage and changed to a nightrobe and dressing

41

gown. She began brushing her hair before a small gilt-framed mirror.

Whatever crisis had occurred among the cattle evidently had been conquered. Matthew and the others had returned a short time earlier. She had looked out and had seen him enter the main room, accompanied by Paul Drexel. Hester had hurried to fill their plates with the food that she had kept warmed.

The familiar task of drawing a comb through her hair soothed Lisa, brought a clarity of mind. She now regretted that she had met Micah Jones' challenge and had accepted the inheritance. If there were debts, they could be taken care of by the courts. She decided that she would pen a refusal in the morning.

But there was the matter of Frank O'Hara's murder. The comb halted. She gazed helplessly at her reflection.

She turned suddenly. In the mirror, she had seen the curtains move at the small window in the east wall. Her heart gave an alarmed leap, but she saw that the night wind was stirring and moving the hangings slightly.

Reassured, she walked to the window. The heavy wooden shutters were open to admit air. She looked out, but could see only the dark outline of trees along the irrigation stream. A waning moon was rising. She returned to the dressing stand.

A hand tapped the door. She started up. "Is it you, Mrs. Barbee?" she called.

The knock was repeated. Taking that as an affirmation, she lifted the wooden bar and opened the door. She had two visitors. Matthew stood in the candlelight. With him was the jaunty, smiling Paul Drexel.

Paul was enjoying the way they had deluded her, but Matthew seemed to be merely curious. They were kindred spirits.

Lisa surmised that she was facing a test at their hands. She became aware that she was outlined against the light, and that the draft through the door was sending her dressing gown swirling. She clutched it tightly around her. She tried to close the door, but Paul blocked it with an outstretched hand.

"Don't worry," he said. "You're modest. Very. That blasted nightgown's got enough foofaraw sewed into it to hide three females. Do you agree, Matt?"

Matthew nodded. "I never could figure why women wear more clothes to bed than they do in public."

"Just what do you want?" Lisa demanded.

"Maybe you'd like to go for a ride to sort of settle you down for a good night's sleep," Paul said.

"Ride? A horseback ride? In the dark?"

"You'd be surprised how well you can see out there," Paul said.

"A million stars," Matthew spoke softly. "A million candles. And soon the moon. And the wind rippling in your hair. Molten beauty against a lake of silver."

"He talks like that quite often," Paul said. "You ought to see some of the stuff he reads."

"You're *both* out of your minds," Lisa said. "I'm getting ready for bed."

"Sleep is for old men and withered women," Matthew said. "At our age there's no time. We own the world now. We must enjoy it while we can. The past is gone beyond recall. You owe it to the future to make the most of the present. The night was made for beauty, the moon for yearning, and the dawn for fulfillment. Dreary rooms and bolted doors are only for loneliness."

"What the boy is trying to say," Paul explained, "is that it would be a hell of a lot of fun."

She eyed them speculatively. She was thinking of the rider she had seen departing from O'Hara House. Even Paul Drexel might have been that man. He was of about the same stature and posture as the two Barbees. It was evident that their tie of comradeship was very close. Perhaps Hester had made a gingham shirt also for Paul Drexel.

But at the moment, the thought suddenly seemed fantastic. Perhaps it was the witchery of the candlelight or the ingenuousness of the two stalwart tempters who stood so ingratiatingly on her doorstep. For the instant at least, she found herself absolving them.

"It's impossible, of course," she said, a trifle weakly.

"Impossible?" Paul demanded. "Why?"

"What would people think?"

"People? Why, they already have their opinion of us. They've got me branded as hell-bent in a handbasket. They think Matt will float away on one of his daydreams some fine afternoon. And their views on you are thrown and branded. Nothing will change that now."

Lisa was interested. "What *are* their views on me?"

Matthew spoke languidly. "They're envious of you, chiefly, my voluminously-clad sprite."

"Envious? Why, they think I'm a mercenary person. A loose woman."

Matthew nodded. "Exactly. And the majority of the females in this range would give ten years of their lives to change places with you."

"That's ridiculous! Why would they want that?"

Matthew reached out and touched her hair. "Your mirror will give you that answer. It isn't often we have the chance to make love to a redheaded beauty. There'll be none, mercenary or otherwise, on the trail to Abilene and beyond, I fear."

Lisa realized that in them was the same seeking for contentment, the same yearning to capture the essence of happiness that was her own burden. They were seeing the emptiness of the journey ahead, the loneliness. This, she understood, was what drove them now. She was young, warm, desirable. They sought only to be near her for a time, to hear her voice, to touch her, to try to win her.

"I'll go," she said abruptly. The decision came from the same reckless phase in her nature that had impelled her to consider accepting the inheritance, a chance-taking urge she had never given in to in the past.

She had a new thought. "What will Abel say?"

Instantly she regretted the question. Her visitors looked at each other. Silence came.

"Where is Abel?" she asked reluctantly.

"With the cattle," Paul Drexel said, and there was savage defeat in him now. "Helping keep them glued on the bedground. Looking after them, singing to them, nursing them along. Like always. Abel's chained to them. Yoked to them, just as he yokes bunch quitters to *cabestros* to tame them."

Matthew sighed. "There goes the fun. There'd be no joy riding with the wind, free and laughing, knowing that Abel's out there, carrying all of the load and counting on me to share it with him."

He kissed Lisa gently on the cheek. "Abel is our conscience. Perhaps there'll be another night and another moon. Maybe Paul won't be in the way. Then I'll make love to you."

"I'll always be in the way," Paul declared.

They bowed and walked away. Lisa stood in the doorway, listening to their receding footsteps. The aroma of the pipe Paul had been smoking lingered around her. That and the elusive, pungent tang of saddle leather and of horseflesh, of grass crushed beneath hooves, and of mesquite and all the wild, growing things that brooded out there in the blackness. And of the cattle.

She retreated reluctantly into her room and closed the door. An owl hooted in the thickets, the sound harshly weird. A cow bawled somewhere far in the hills.

Lisa was still holding the comb in her hand. She finished with her hair. She turned back the coverlet on the bed. The moon had swung high, so that its light framed the window. She threw off the dressing gown and pushed back the window curtains to admit the cooling air. She walked to the stand to extinguish the candles.

The roar of a pistol shot filled the room with sound and glare and powdersmoke. The post on the bedstead at her side was splintered by a bullet. The concussion blew out the candles.

Lisa scrambled to shelter, crouching beyond the bed, her terrified eyes on the open window. Someone had stood out there in the darkness and had tried to kill her in the same manner Frank O'Hara had been slain.

She screamed. She heard Hester lift a response. Men's voices arose. Feet pounded. Lisa wrapped the robe around her and opened the door for them.

Matthew was there, and Paul Drexel, wearing only breeches and boots. Micah Jones, along with other riders, came racing from the bunkhouse. Hester, bundled in a cloak, arrived.

Lisa chattered an explanation and the men hurried away to scan the surroundings. But there was a hard-packed footpath along the east wall, beneath the window where the assailant had stood, which yielded no bootprints.

Matthew led a search of the brush beyond the house, without result. After half an hour all the men came back.

"Any idea who did it?" Matthew asked.

"Yes," Lisa said. "The same man who killed Frank O'Hara."

"Why would he want to kill you too?" Matthew asked slowly.

Lisa had no answer for that. Hester placed an arm around her, patting her on the shoulder. "We'll find out who it was, Elizabeth. I'll fix up a cup of tea to settle our nerves. I've got a pinch of it left. Been savin' it for an occasion. Matthew an' Paul will get their blankets an' sleep outside your door an' window the rest of the night. This won't happen ag'in, I'll guarantee."

Lisa watched the competent hands of Hester brew and pour the tea. She was thinking that those hands had taken the life of a Comanche. She was wondering if they also had been capable of firing a pistol with intent to kill a girl. Perhaps it had been a woman, not a man, outside her window. Would maternal protectiveness drive a mother that far?

Afterward, in her room, Lisa barred her door and moved the highboy against it. She wedged the prayer bench into the window alcove.

She did not sleep for hours. The wind died. She could hear the steady breathing of Matthew and Paul, who slept outside the walls of her room.

Abel evidently was still with the herd. But it was not far

away. A man could have ridden near the house, stolen in on foot to that window and returned to his horse. No one would be able to say that he had ever left the cattle at all.

She slept intermittently. She heard the bunkhouse occupants astir at dawn. She arose, dragged the highboy away and opened the door. Matthew's bedroll was empty. He and Paul Drexel were dousing their faces in a wash trough at the bunkhouse, along with other men.

A jovial, brawny Negro cook, with a deep, resonant voice, was hurrying with breakfast preparations in the cookhouse, which was a part of the bunkshed. As long as the herd was held so near at hand, the more comfortable quarters at the ranch were being used as the base of operations.

Paul waved to her. All of them hurried to eat. Soon they were roping horses at the corral. Lisa shrank from the violence of it. These animals were as wild and undisciplined as the cattle. For a time the ranch yard was filled with leaping, pitching cowponies that were hoping to unseat shouting, impatient men.

One horse, squealing, plunged backwards, trying to pin a leathery-faced vaquero. The man left the saddle at the precise instant to escape injury, followed the movement of his mount as it rolled, and stepped into the stirrups and rose into the saddle again as the animal lurched to its feet. Lisa noticed that the cornhusk cigarette in the vaquero's lips was undisturbed.

"Thet claybank's goin' to ketch you not lookin' some day, Ygnacio, an' run thet saddlehorn right through yore gizzard," one of the riders commented.

"He likes his fun in the morning, Señor Tom," Ygnacio said. "He does not try to keel me. It is only his leetle joke. He could keel me any time he so wanted, in popping the brush. But in the *brasada* he is very, very careful of my life—and also his own. I let him have his fun here where it does no harm, yes?"

The confusion ended abruptly. The animals resigned themselves to the inevitable. Then all of them were gone, galloping to the herd, leaving only a thin haze of dust quivering in the first rays of the rising sun.

Hester called Lisa to breakfast. Hester looked drawn and worn. "Abel will be in soon," she said. "He stayed all night with the cattle."

Presently three tired riders came in and turned their horses into the feed corral. One was Abel. The others headed for the cookhouse, and he walked to the main house. He was saddle-stiff and marked by lack of sleep as he came into the room.

He wasted no words. "Matt an' the others told me all they know about what happened last night. I——"

"It can wait, son," Hester interrupted. "You better get some sleep. Elizabeth can talk to you later."

"I've lost sleep before," he said. "An' will ag'in." He looked at Lisa. "Tell me anythin' you might have recollected since it happened. Tell me everythin'."

Lisa repeated the meager details.

He said, "Show me."

He led the way to her room. "Where was you standin'?"

Lisa walked to the dressing table. "Here."

He left the room and strode to the east side of the house. He peered in the small window, pointing his finger in simulation of aiming a pistol. Presently he returned.

"He had to shoot mainly by guess," he said. "All he could see was your reflection in thet mirror. Maybe thet's why he missed at such close range. But maybe he was only tryin' to skeer you."

"Scare me? For what purpose?"

"Your guess is as good as mine."

"It was more than trying to scare me," Lisa said. "He meant to kill me. The bullet barely missed me. What can I do?"

Able shrugged. "You could light a shuck out'n this country an' go back no'th."

Lisa stiffened. "Perhaps that's what this person wants. Or persons."

Abel gazed at her. "Persons wearin' checked shirts, you mean?"

She did not have to answer that, for he turned and walked out of the room and down the gallery to the family eating room. Hester hurried after him to provide his breakfast.

Afterward Lisa heard him enter his own quarters in the adjoining section of the house. The door closed. She listened to the thud of a boot being hurled against a wall. She remembered that volcanic moment of frustration and protest when he had smashed the empty whiskey jug in the littered bunkhouse.

Through a window she saw Hester standing in the door of the main room. Hester had heard that sound also. Seeing Lisa gazing, Hester withdrew, but not before Lisa clearly saw the anguish in her face—anguish for a son whose burden she wanted to lighten, but could not.

Lisa looked at the little shrine in her room. It typified the soothing peace of this stronghold. More and more, she understood the sorrow that was in Hester at the necessity of leaving this place. And more and more also, she was aware of the resistless factor that was forcing this move upon the Barbees. The cattle! The living, breathing cattle. These, after all, were the bone and sinew of the Bar B, its lifeblood, its reason for existence.

Nothing must stand in the way of survival of the herd. The herd was Bar B, not this house where all of the sons had been born, or even the land. Parting with these memories would be hard, but part they would if it were for the sake of the cattle.

It was clear that the responsibility was entirely on Abel's shoulders. Hester shrank from uprooting themselves and delving into the unknown. Matthew was content to abide by the judgment of his elder brother.

Abel made all the vital decisions. Perhaps he could even decide life or death for a man who stood in their way—or a woman.

Lisa made up her mind to leave Monte Vista. It had been a mistake to accept Barbee hospitality, suspecting Abel of murder, as she did. An almost fatal mistake, apparently.

She found Hester back at the task of sorting and packing belongings for the journey. "I'm thankful for your kindness, Mrs. Barbee," she said, "but I believe it best to move to Triangle O, at least for the time I am owner."

Hester nodded. "I expected you'd look at it that way. I'll have Micah drive you over. He's still around."

As Micah was loading her luggage into the wagon, a top buggy from San Ysidro arrived. It brought Sam Miller and Kemp Travis.

Travis alighted. "Good afternoon, Elizabeth," he said, beaming. He looked around. "I see that you're moving out. To Triangle O, no doubt. Micah, there's no need for you to go to that trouble. I'll drive Miss Randolph over. Sam has some legal issues to discuss with her and a few papers to sign. I've a matter or two I want to take up with her."

Travis had a hand on her arm and was turning her toward the wagon. He had a talent for physically forcing persons into the paths he wanted them to follow. Lisa held back, compelling him to halt.

Abel appeared on the gallery. Evidently he had just awakened, for he was still stuffing in the tail of his shirt. It was the checked gingham shirt, freshly washed and ironed. It was plain that he had chosen to wear it in arrogance and defiance of her unspoken accusation against him.

He came toward them with his long stride. "One of these things you-all want to take up with Miss Randolph wouldn't be an offer to buy up what beef cattle Frank owned, now would it, Kemp?" he asked.

"That," Travis said, "is none of your concern, Abel."

"About five and half a head is what you're aimin' to throw out as bait, I reckon," Abel said easily.

"That's more than they're worth hereabouts right now," Travis shrugged.

Abel spoke to Lisa. "Don't be hasty."

"All this is entirely out of place, and mercenary," Lisa said angrily. "Frank O'Hara has been in his grave less than a day."

"Runnin' cattle gits to be a mighty rough business," Abel said. "You ought to know thet by this time. Frank ain't the first man thet's had a herd sold right over his grave. Won't be the last, either."

"I will not discuss any such matter today," Lisa said. "Why, I'm not even the legal owner. There must be formalities."

Abel nodded. "I reckon they've been took care of. That's why Kemp's brought Sam here so early in the mornin'."

Sam Miller spoke nervously. "After all, it's only a routine affair. Court is in session at San Ysidro. The will is clear and sound. Mr. O'Hara named you administratrix. I've arranged for court approval of a bond so that you are fully empowered to manage the estate and conduct business until you come into formal legal title, which will be very shortly, I'm sure. There are no O'Hara heirs living. Even if there were, the will is unassailable. I guarantee that."

"Didn't I tell you?" Abel told Lisa. "Kemp has greased the skids."

Travis ignored Abel. "As a matter of fact, I do intend to make an offer to buy Triangle O beef from you, Elizabeth."

"At five and a half, jest like I said?" Abel jeered.

"A fair price," Travis snapped.

"You heard me say the other day thet cattle might sell at double thet price up no'th," Abel said to Lisa. "Maybe more."

"I'm offering cash, not fool's hopes," Travis said. "It's a long, hard trail to the railroad. Plenty of cattle never make it." He added, "Plenty of men, too."

"I will talk over your offer some other time, Mr. Travis," Lisa said.

"Both offers?" he demanded quickly.

She knew what he meant. She met his gaze squarely. "No," she said. "Only the one in regard to buying cattle."

"You'll reconsider," Travis said confidently.

"There's no need for you and Mr. Miller going all the way to O'Hara House," she said. "I can sign any papers here."

Abel spoke to Lisa. "You ain't as addle-brained as I took

you to be," he said grudgingly. "Don't let him soft-talk you into changin' yore mind—about sellin' steers at his price, I mean."

He walked back to his room to resume his interrupted rest.

Travis reached for his cigar case. There was raw anger in his eyes. He had been blocked by Abel, for the time at least, and was forced to accept that fact.

"Get the papers signed, Sam," he said tersely. "We'll head back to town."

CHAPTER 8

Darkness had come again. Lisa sat in crowded sleeping quarters at Triangle O, with writing paper before her on a small plank table which was slung to the wall on hinges.

Micah Jones had driven her to the ranch in mid-afternoon. The ruins of O'Hara House on the knoll still gave forth a few spirals of smoke. The odor of charred wood hung in the night.

She was not alone on the place. A Mexican woman, bosomy and with a prominent gold tooth in the middle of her smiling countenance, had appeared, driving a rickety wagon. She was accompanied by a horseman—a small, wiry vaquero constructed apparently of rawhide stretched loosely over a durable frame.

"I am Rosalia, *si,*" the woman had said. "Thees ees Mario Rojas, my hoosband, *mi esposo.*"

Lisa knew they had been sent by Hester to look after her. She had rather resented their presence, but now, with the darkness of this brushy land imprisoning her, she was grateful that they were on hand.

Rosalia and her husband were quartered in the huge bunkhouse. Lisa occupied a small lean-to, adjoining the cookhouse, where Triangle O cooks had lived. Rosalia had helped her scrub and dust and make the place livable.

Lisa had hoped that Micah Jones would stay, but he had driven away, heading for Monte Vista, after seeing that she was settled. "There'll be somebody over from Bar B before dark to help keep an eye on things," he had told her. "Mario and Rosalia will always be within call. You won't be alone."

Her decision to go to Triangle O had been a bit of bravado, a display of independence of Hester. She knew now it would have been better to have returned to San Ysidro and taken accommodations there until she could definitely decide her future.

She was writing a letter to an acquaintance in Chicago. Pretending to write, rather. She hardly knew what words she had set down. It was a letter she did not expect to finish. She was merely trying to keep her mind occupied.

She was frightened. Every sound—and there were many as the cookhouse contracted in the cooling evening—caused her to listen tensely. She found her teeth locked so tightly that her jaws were beginning to ache. These creakings echoed in empty spaces, for the cookhouse, like all the O'Hara projects, had been laid out in a grand size that had never been fully utilized.

She started up as she heard a rider approaching. The arrival came into the ranch yard and called out, "All right, Mario. Rosalia!"

It was Abel Barbee's voice. Lisa's heart gave a thud. She gazed around with a trapped sensation. She had blocked the door and the window in the small room with benches in the same way she had barricaded herself in at Monte Vista after the attempt on her life.

Mario's response to Abel was in Spanish. The two talked in the yard for a moment. Mario went back into the bunkhouse. She could hear Abel approaching the cookhouse.

"Miss Randolph! It's Abel Barbee."

She debated it. Finally she opened the door and entered the echoing cookhouse. The streaming fan of light from the oil lamp that burned in the smaller room formed a path for her. She was keenly conscious of the somber shadows on either hand.

Abel stood waiting at the outer door, faintly reached by the light. She saw that he must have come directly from working with the cattle, for he still wore his leather leggings and the hat with the chin strap.

"Evenin'," he said. "I had aimed on gettin' here before dark, but I run across a flitterrear in the shinnery thet had been too smart for the circle riders to ketch. I busted him an' wrangled him back to the bedground."

"I see," Lisa commented.

He chuckled. "I don't reckon you savvy what I'm talkin' about, do you?"

"I believe so," she said. "You caught another cow. Did you sew its eyes closed?"

He flushed. "No," he said tersely. He eyed her. "Scared?" he asked.

She did not attempt to evade. "A little."

"You shouldn't have come here. You'd be better off at Monte Vista where we could watch over you."

When she made no comment, he asked, "Got a pistol?"

"A pistol? No."

He was carrying a holstered weapon and had a second firearm thrust in his belt. He produced this pistol and offered it to her. "I brought it along to give to you."

She drew away from it. "I wouldn't have the least notion how to use it."

"This is a .44," he explained. "Heavy for a lady, but easy to fire. It stops what you slam down on—if'n you aim straight. You pull back the hammer this way."

He moved into the cookhouse into better light and demonstrated. "Then you jest point the barr'l an' pull the trigger. Like pointin' your finger."

Lisa was a little breathless. "I never had anything bigger than a tiny target pistol in my hand in my life."

"There's a sayin' thet a person might need a shootin' piece only once in his time, but when he does he shore needs it mighty bad." He placed the pistol in her hands.

Its weight startled her. She held it with both hands. He eyed her dubiously. "Maybe you was right when you said you never had a real pistol in yore hand," he observed. "Or you're purty good at pretendin'."

She understood his meaning. The boldness of it angered her. He was as much as telling her that she, not he, was the one who was under suspicion as Frank O'Hara's murderer.

He walked away. "Good night!" he said. "I'll stay around an' sleep light. Curtain your window an' keep the door locked."

Lisa retreated to the lean-to. She stood gripping the pistol. She had a suffocating sensation. Holding the weapon gingerly, she carefully placed it in a drawer in the scarred washstand and closed it tightly.

She barricaded the door. She heard Abel talking to Rosalia and Mario, but the conversation was in Spanish.

Mario said, *"Buenas noches, mi amigo."*

Lisa heard Abel ride away. After an interval she understood that Mario and Rosalia had turned in for the night.

Silence came, and she was once again aware of the creaking and complaining of the dry joints of the building. She got into her nightgown, blew out the lamp and crept into the musty-odored bunk. She lay tense and quivering.

Finally she arose. Feeling her way in the dark she lifted the pistol from the drawer and placed it beneath her pillow. She was certain she would never have the courage to fire at a human being. Still, its presence offered a measure of reassurance.

She drifted into sleep.

The heavy report of a gun brought her awake and out of the bunk. She crouched in the center of the room in darkness.

Another shot came, followed by three or four more in overlapping din. The concussions rattled the door.

She could hear a man running fast in the yard. She moved to the window, pulled aside the chair she had wedged there and lifted the cloth she had hung as a curtain.

The moon, a tarnished half-disk, washed the scene with faint light. She could see only the vacancy of the shadowed ranch yard and the black shapes of the buildings.

Mario shouted something in Spanish in the bunkhouse. Abel's voice responded from somewhere beyond the house. He spoke in English, evidently for Lisa's benefit. "All of you stay where you are. We don't want to be shootin' at each other."

The pound of hooves of a fast-moving horse arose. Pistols began firing, the exchange moving swiftly away in the direction of the corral.

A lull came and she could again make out the rattle of hooves. The rider was escaping. Two more shots came from a distance in the brush. That ended the firing.

Lisa cleared the door, unbarred it and raced through the cookhouse into the open. Mario emerged from the bunkhouse, clad only in his breeches and carrying a pistol. "Go back, *señorita!*" he implored.

He ran toward the brush. Lisa followed, barefoot, her nightrobe flying. Mario passed the buildings and the corral. Scattered mesquite loomed ahead. He was barefoot also, and both he and Lisa were suffering from thorns and rocks.

Lisa discovered that she was carrying the pistol Abel had given her. She hadn't remembered snatching it up.

She sighted another figure ahead. It was Abel. Mario joined him and she also moved up.

A dead horse lay in the brush. Lisa moved to Abel's side. The animal bore a saddle and bridle. Mario and Abel bent closer, peering.

They straightened and Abel looked at Lisa. "I reckon even a greenhorn like you kin read a brand that plain," he said. "That's a Bar B horse. It's a roan from my own string. Maybe you remember it? It was the horse I was ridin' the day you tried to use a whip on me for lid-sewin' thet *ladino*."

"The saddle, *amigo?*" Mario questioned reluctantly.

"Mine too," Abel said slowly. "It's an old hull I kept in the jockey shed at Monte Vista for emergency use. The roan had been worked pretty hard lately, and I turned him out in the fenced pasture above the ranch yesterday."

He raced away and Lisa heard him mount his horse, which he had left in hiding in the wagon shed. He spurred away into the brush.

"It weel be no use," Mario told Lisa. "Many, many men could hide in the thickets at night on foot and never be seen."

He was right. Abel returned after a time. He had abandoned the search as futile. "I pretended to leave when I first came here," he explained to Lisa. "But I came back and hung around. I was afeared the person who took thet shot at you last night might make a second try. I heard a horse out in the brush, an' waited. I glimpsed someone injunin' toward the cookhouse on foot. I circled the place, aimin' to take him by surprise, but I bumped into a double-damned rain barr'l an' he heard me. He didn't waste time. He started shootin' an' lit a shuck. I smoked him up as he was ridin', but it looks like all thet I hit was the horse."

He did not speak for a time. "You don't believe me, do you?" he demanded grimly.

"Did you see this man?"

"Got one glimpse o' him in the moonlight, but he was huggin' the neck of his horse an' I couldn't make out much about him."

Again a long silence. Abel Barbee could have planned it all, Lisa told herself. It could have been merely another attempt to confuse her and cover his own guilt in both the death of Frank O'Hara and the attempt on her life the previous night.

He could have left the roan horse in the thickets, staged a false pistol fight and slain the animal himself.

Then too there was always the possibility that Matthew might be the guilty one and that he had been the intruder, either with or without Abel's knowledge.

"There's only one thing I'm sure of," Abel said. "He wasn't wearin' a blue an' white check shirt—this time."

Lisa turned abruptly and went back to her quarters in the cookhouse. She barred the door of the lean-to, but did not barricade it or the window.

Again anger ran in her. If there really had been an intruder, his purpose had been to frighten her or kill her. She suddenly realized that she was no longer afraid. Not the sort of fear she had known when she first had faced the roughness of this land, at least. There was apprehension in her, full and healthy in its desire to live, but there was also resentment and a determination to strike back if the opportunity came.

She got into bed. She reached beneath the pillow and pulled the heavy pistol to a better position where she could seize it up quickly.

The thought that perhaps she was being tricked caused her to start up. Was the weapon really loaded? She lifted it in both hands, eared back the hammer, aimed at the roof, closed her eyes and pulled the trigger . . . and blew a neat round hole in the shingles. Dust sifted down upon her.

She heard Abel and Mario come running. "It's all right!" she called out. "I was just trying out the pistol to see if it worked."

"Tryin' it out?" Abel snorted. "You liked to have skeered me knock-kneed."

But she sensed that he knew why she had tested the firearm, for he offered no further criticism. He and Mario went away, mumbling.

She sank back on the bed and placed the pistol handy again. "Just like pointing your fingers," she murmured, satisfied.

On that stern thought, she fell soundly asleep. Even the creaking of the building and the drive of the wind, which always seemed to blow hard at midnight in this region, did not awaken her.

CHAPTER 9

It was sunup when she swung her legs out of the bunk. Memory returned. The events of the night seemed unreal and fanciful. As she dressed she was touched by a satisfaction as she realized she was rested and ready to face a new day. The anger was still in her, warming her.

She removed the improvised curtain at the window. The sun was just peering over the farthest rim. In this slanting light the brush country stretched, ridge upon ridge, like the waves of the sea southward, mile after mile. It formed an exquisite pattern of mauve and lilac and purple shadows and golden-crested summits.

Its wild magnificence brought an exhilaration that carried her to emotional heights. Along with that was almost a sorrow, a realization that this was something of which no human could ever be really a part. There was a wild longing in her to capture this beauty and preserve it forever, but there was also the deadening knowledge that this could never be.

Movement nearer at hand caught her attention. Abel Barbee appeared on foot from the mesquite and came walking past the corral and to the ranch yard. He carried a rifle in addition to his six-shooter.

He paused and stood, lank and solemn, gazing at the same beauty that had held her. It came to her that he was torn between the same conflict of spiritual rejoicing and sadness.

He turned and saw that she was watching him. He walked nearer and spoke. "I've been out in the shinnery since first light. It's my guess the fella had a second horse staked at a distance on which he lit out. The country's full o' tracks made by us brush poppers chousin' the cattle."

There was nothing Lisa could say that would not sound disbelieving or accusing. She retreated from the window and entered the cookhouse. She was confronted by dust and rust. The size of the fireplace and the equipment appalled her. Rosalia, however, seemed right at home. She found utensils more suitable for their purpose. There was a scant food supply and coffee beans for grinding. Breakfast was soon ready.

Abel and Mario appeared when Rosalia pounded on the iron wagon rim which hung outside the door. Rosalia imperiously motioned Lisa to take her place at the head of the table.

Lisa gazed helplessly down the length of the huge board and slid onto the bench, feeling childishly small and entirely inadequate.

"Room for everybody an' two dozen more," Abel said as he and Mario seated themselves.

Rosalia brought food, and Mario ate swiftly and hurried away to saddle up for the day's work. Lisa and Abel finished their own breakfast in silence.

"Quite a number of persons were employed by Mr. O'Hara in the past, evidently," Lisa ventured.

"As high as thirty riders durin' roundup," Abel said. "Thet was in his father's time."

"How many now?" Lisa asked.

"Mario's the last of the crew. Even the cook quit months ago. Mario has been helpin' us with the Bar B roundup. Rosalia had gone over to Bar B, too, to stay with Chepita, who is her cousin. Thet's why nobody but Frank was here the day you first came to O'Hara House."

"You said there were cattle? Quite a number, apparently."

"Beef ain't worth much out in the *brasada*. Nor anywhere else from the way it looks."

"*Brasada?*"

"I keep forgittin' you're a greenhorn. Thet means shinnery. Chaparral. Thickets! Understand?"

"I see."

"You don't see. You don't know a cussed thing about this country, or about cattle!"

"Why should I?" Lisa demanded angrily.

"You own cattle. Maybe more'n you realize. Frank hasn't rounded up T O beef in two, three years. Too much work, an' no profit anyway. But we've picked up close to six hundred head of prime T O steers, along with our Bar B stuff. We're holdin' 'em in the bunch. There're still a lot more between here an' the Rio Conejo. Thet's a stream about twenty miles south. Triangle O used to keep drift camps down there."

"Drift camps?"

"What do you keer what a drift camp is?" he snapped. "You said you didn't keer anythin' about cattle."

"The word," she said, trying to shatter his assurance, "is 'care,' not 'keer.' And I did not say I don't care anything about cattle. If I own as many as you seem to think, it's best that I learn something about them. Now tell me. What are these drift camps?"

"Line camps where cowboys stay an' shove driftin' cattle back to their proper range," he said. "Now I don't *keer* a plugged penny whether you learn anythin' about cattle or not, but I'm willin' to put up a business deal with you."

"What is it?" Lisa demanded.

"The same one Frank welched on when he thought he was goin' to get married."

She glared at him. "So that *was* the reason you fought with him! You knew that first day we met, when you were torturing that poor cow, that—that I was the woman. He had told you."

He nodded. "Yeah. I knew you was the one."

"What sort of a deal would be so important that you'd— you'd—fight with a friend?" she asked. "He was your friend, wasn't he?"

His gaze was hard to endure. "You tried to say I killed Frank, but you couldn't quite bring yourself to it. Why? If you believe it, say it."

Lisa matched his bluntness. "You seem to be the only one who had cause. You could have ridden to O'Hara House after meeting me that day on the road. You might have had another row with Mr. O'Hara, because you knew for sure that the woman who was the cause of his welching, as you call it, actually existed and had arrived. And perhaps you had other reasons."

"Don't forgit thet some folks think you did it," he reminded her.

"But the real facts point to you," she said.

He eyed her thoughtfully. "I wasn't within two miles of O'Hara House thet day. But it's only my word ag'in yours."

"It's more than just my word," she said.

He nodded. "You mean the checked shirt. Hester didn't tell me about thet 'til after the inquest."

"But she told Matthew," Lisa said. "She had him dress up in one just like it that day."

Again he nodded. He spoke, without change of tone. "It could have been me, or it could have been Matt. I talked to the ridin' crew. Matt was poppin' brush all afternoon an' was workin' alone. Nobody but him could say where he was or what he did."

"It seems to be between the two of you and myself," Lisa said.

"An' this fella who stole my horse an' saddle to ride over here last night," he said, and she saw a headstrong anger in him.

"What was this business deal you mentioned?" she asked.

He made a tired gesture. "We sorta got off that track, didn't we? I reckon there's no use even talkin' about it."

"I'm curious."

"Frank had agreed to throw in with Bar B," he said. "Cash money is what we need when we move no'th. It takes a stake to establish a ranch. There're supplies to buy, payrolls to meet, buildin's to put up. Maybe we'll have to buy land. Above all, we need blooded stock. Pedigreed bulls an' top-grade heifers. I aim to go into Herefords. I can see the end of the day of the Longhorn as a beef critter. Our Bar B ain't goin' to tally out more'n around eighteen hundred head of beeves. With Frank as partner, we could have gone to market with close to three thousand. If prices are as low as last season we'd still be in trouble, but could scratch through. But we're roundin' up early. I aimed to be there ahead of the crowd an' have a better chance at a good price."

He quit talking for a moment. "Then Frank backed out," he said.

"What about Kemp Travis's offer?" she asked.

"Jest why he's in such a sweat to buy, I don't know," he admitted. "Smells a profit somewhere. Thet's for sure. He offered to buy from Frank under the same terms. Frank wouldn't sell. Frank never liked Kemp. Frank was the kind of a man thet if he didn't like you he wouldn't have any truck with you at all."

"Would you be any better off, leaving Texas?" she asked.

"In addition to hard times," he said, "we're losin' grass. Mesquite's runnin' us out. Hester'll tell you thet when she an' my Dad built Monte Vista there was grass clearings it took half an hour to ride across. Even I remember, as a boy, when Frank's house overlooked mainly prairie where cattle got fat an' was easy to round up. Now look at it. The brush is right up to the corrals. Monte Vista's the same way. The mesquite keeps movin' in. The country gits dryer. Each year brush-poppin' gits tougher on a man. The steers grow meaner an' harder to ketch. Rattlesnakes, wild pigs an' outlaws. They're takin' over. There's the prickly pear. It's beginnin' to cover square miles. An' the huisache is a bush thet's as bad as the mesquite."

"Where is this new country you want to move to?" Lisa asked.

"Wyomin', or maybe Dakota. Maybe even as fur as Montana. It's free grass, but cattlemen are beginnin' to move in. Another year or two an' the best of it'll be taken."

He repeated it. "Free grass! Open prairie an' plains. I seen it once. Went up the trail with a herd to Abilene an' took a ride of my own on no'th. There it was, a whole big world of it."

There was a shining eagerness in him. "No brush to eat out a man's heart or pen him in like he was in jail."

He came back to reality. He smiled. "Sounded a little like Matt that time, didn't I?" he remarked sheepishly.

"This free grass is far away," Lisa said. "It must be terribly difficult and dangerous to get there."

"If anythin's worth the havin', it's worth the tryin'."

"What were the terms of this agreement you had with Mr. O'Hara?"

"Frank was to share in the outfit an' in the profits in proportion to the cattle each had at the start. He was to have equal say in any decisions."

"It was a contract, I assume?"

"In writin'? We didn't figure it was necessary. A man's word ought to be good."

He seemed to brace himself, then said tersely, "An' besides, I kain't read or write very good."

He saw the look in her eyes. Titanic resentment flamed in him. "I want none o' your pity!" he exploded.

He walked to the corral. Without another glance in her direction he saddled up and rode away in the direction of Monte Vista.

CHAPTER 10

Lisa stood watching Abel Barbee appear and reappear on the trail as it hurdled the brushy ridges, until distance had taken him for good.

She gazed at the ashes of O'Hara House, and the remaining structures and the encroaching brush. She had inherited a dying ranch. Rosalia, washing dishes in the cookhouse, was watching her through a window. She realized that she must appear ludicrous, standing there, holding the hem of her skirt out of the dust. She knew the dismal depths of a sense of utter inadequacy.

She walked into the cookhouse, picked up a floursack towel, and began drying the dishes.

Rosalia spoke suddenly. "They are good people, the Barbees, yes. I would do what the *caporal* says."

"The *caporal?*"

"Señor Abel. He ees *caporal*. What you call the chief one. The leader."

Leader? A man who admitted he could barely read or write?

The sound of trotting hooves brought her to the window. Sam Miller's buggy was approaching. Riding saddleback ahead of it was Kemp Travis on a sleek red horse.

She met them in the ranch yard. Travis took her hand in both of his and let his gaze rove admiringly over her. "You're a very comely woman, Elizabeth."

Lisa withdrew her hand. "I'll warm coffee and have Rosalia get something for you to eat."

"Coffee only," Travis said. "Sam has more papers for you to sign. Afterwards, I want to talk to you, if I may."

"Surely," Lisa said. Sam Miller produced a leather satchel and she led him into the bunkhouse. Travis preferred to remain outside, smoking a cigar.

The lawyer opened his satchel and laid out legal documents. "They're to be examined by you and signed in connection with the probate," he said. "They will have to be attested, of course, and witnessed."

He brought out another sheaf of papers. "Now to take up another matter. Do you know, Miss Randolph, that Triangle O—or rather Frank O'Hara—was heavily in debt?"

"Micah Jones mentioned it," Lisa said. "In fact it was one of the reasons I accepted the ranch."

"Well, well!" Sam Miller exclaimed. He looked at her with sudden new respect. His task seemed lighter.

"What are the debts?" Lisa asked.

"For one thing, Frank has failed to pay his county tax in the last three years," the lawyer explained. "And he signed some personal notes at the bank in San Ysidro when he was in need of cash. There are overdue bills at the general store and other establishments. But the biggest single item is in IOU's."

He looked over his glasses at her. "The IOU's are mainly gambling debts. You can ignore them, of course. They would have no legal standing as a claim against the estate."

"How much do they come to?" Lisa asked.

"More than eight thousand dollars."

Lisa was shocked. "He lost all that gambling?"

Miller shrugged. "Frank never played a penny ante game, unfortunately. The other legal obligations, including the promissory notes, taxes and store accounts, amount to more than six thousand dollars. A few more probably will show up."

Lisa pored through the sheaf of papers. Some of the IOU's were stained with water rings made by liquor glasses. One was written on a scrap of buckskin that apparently had been cut from some person's hunting skirt.

"Notify everyone interested that these will be paid off if it is at all possible," she said. "It will take time, of course. Considerable time. Perhaps years."

"Even the gambling debts?" Miller asked incredulously.

"The other obligations will be taken care of first, of course," Lisa said. "But the IOU's will be paid, if possible, provided the money was lost fairly."

"Oh, I guess the games were fair enough," Miller said. "Frank was a fool when it came to playing poker. You will note that a man named Coe Slade is the holder of several of these items in considerable amounts. He is Kemp Travis's bodyguard."

"Bodyguard?"

Miller glanced nervously around to make sure Travis was not within earshot, and lowered his voice. "Let us say he works for Kemp."

"I see," Lisa said. "He'll be paid if he is entitled to the money."

Miller shuffled the papers nervously for a moment.

"There's one other matter," he said hesitantly. "It, also, is not legally binding, but I happen to know that Frank had borrowed considerable money from the Barbees from time to time. He had been able to pay little or nothing back."

Lisa straightened. "How much is it?"

"Nearly ten thousand dollars, I'm afraid. At least that was what Frank estimated it to be. He told me about it when he had me draw up his will. It was a debt that he meant to pay. Of that I'm sure."

Lisa was appalled. "Ten thousand dollars? Good grief! Do you realize that all this comes to nearly twenty-five thousand dollars?"

"I do," Miller nodded. "And that is more than Triangle O is worth right now. Considerably more, I'm afraid."

He evidently expected her to break into a storm of chagrined denunciation. His expression caused Lisa to laugh. "Well, at least my conscience is soothed," she said. "I didn't feel right about taking the inheritance. As it stands, there really isn't any inheritance at all."

"As I said, the gambling debts and this obligation to the Barbees are not binding," Miller hastened to say.

"Do you mean there are no records of the loans the Barbees made?" Lisa demanded. "No notes?"

"No. That's the way it always was with the Barbees and the O'Haras. Any other way would have been considered an insult. The money was loaned to Frank to meet his taxes and payrolls and store bills. The Barbees thought that's what he was using it for. Instead, he drank and gambled it away."

"But they've never said a word."

"They wouldn't. They're proud. They'll never mention it to you, I'm sure. Or to anyone."

Miller gathered up the papers. "A lot of people, including the bank, will be mighty happy to hear that you want to honor these obligations. Just how you are going to go about raising that much money I wouldn't know."

He arose to leave. "I admire your honesty, Miss Randolph. And I admired Frank, too, in many ways. His sins were the kind that can be forgiven."

He left with Lisa the belief that he could be trusted.

Kemp Travis came in, tossing away his cigar. He seated himself beside her and let his hand rest familiarly on her shoulder. When he saw the look on her face, he withdrew it.

He laughed. "Attractive and also virtuous. Both are rare qualities."

He leaned closer. "Elizabeth, I will pay six dollars a head for all Triangle O beeves, four years and older, that we can round up in a week's time. My estimate is that it will amount to more than a thousand steers. The Barbees already have quite a bunch of T O cattle in their holdout."

He paused, watching her. When she said nothing, he resumed. "Maybe you can guess why I'm being so careless with my money. I'll never really lose it. I look on it as keeping it in the family."

"Are you buying cattle?" Lisa asked. "Or me?"

"You can't turn down an offer like that," he said. "Ask anyone."

"Abel Barbee, for instance?"

His affability vanished. "Abel's a fool. He's going to lose what little the Barbees have left with this gamble up north."

Lisa suddenly made a decision. "I hope not, because the Barbees and I are in this together."

Travis surged to his feet. "Together? Since when?"

"Since just now," she said. "Abel Barbee offered me the same agreement he and Frank O'Hara had reached. I've decided to accept it."

Travis was dangerously furious. "You mean you just decided? Why?"

"The Barbees seem to think there's no future in this region," she said. "And I agree."

"I'll pay you seven dollars a head," he said. "And I'll round up the cattle with my own men. You'll have seven or eight thousand dollars clear profit in your hand within a week."

"From what I hear, cattle haven't been worth the cost of rounding up," she said. "Just why are you so willing to pay that much for them?"

"I've already told you that reason," he said, smiling.

"You will only be disappointed," she said. "I'm sorry."

He understood now that her answer was final. All the tolerant humor was gone from him. He was hostile, suddenly unrelenting.

"The offer still stands," he said, "provided you say nothing to the Barbees about the amount. Naturally I expect to make a profit. A small one."

"By the same way Abel Barbee hopes to make money in cattle?" she asked. "In northern market? You're being inconsistent. You told him the odds were against it."

He shrugged. "Abel is only shooting at the moon. My target is more practical. I'll have my crew at T O in the morning to start rounding up beef."

"No," Lisa said. "I'll stand by my other pledge."

"Pledge? But you said you had made up your mind only this minute to join in with the Barbees."

"That's a pledge," Lisa said. "To myself."

His voice roughened. "You know, of course, that you're throwing in with the man who killed Frank O'Hara. How is that going to look to other people?"

"I don't know about other people. I want to make sure for myself—one way or another. That's why I decided as I did."

He arose angrily. "Maybe you'll both hang from the same gallows!"

He walked to the door and spoke back. "Seven dollars a head, Elizabeth. You'll get no better profit from Abel Barbee in dollars. And none at all in the other matter."

He shouted, "I'm leaving, Sam!" He mounted and galloped up the trail, spurring his horse harshly.

Sam Miller looked at Lisa and said, "You might do better listening to him, Miss Randolph. He's a man who can do a lot of damage if he sets his mind to it."

The lawyer drove away in the dusty wake of the fast-traveling Travis. Both rider and buggy and the dust faded in the distance. But a new plume of dust appeared up the road and drew nearer. It was made by a buckboard with a bay mare in harness. The lone occupant was Hester.

Lisa waited in the ranch yard. Hester obviously was uncertain what her welcome would be as she alighted and said, "I came over to see if I could be of any help. I brought some wild plum preserves thet I put up last fall. Can't take them with me anyway when we pull out."

Lisa led her into the bunkhouse. "Thank you. Mr. Miller and Mr. Travis just left. You probably passed them."

Hester nodded. "Kemp acted like he'd set down on some prickly pear."

"He again offered to buy cattle from this ranch," Lisa said. "He said he'd pay seven dollars a head, provided I didn't tell the Barbees how much he was offering."

"Seven? Mercy! Now, why in the world would Kemp go that high?"

"There was a string attached," Lisa said. "He also wants to marry me."

"I see," Hester sniffed. "Thet's Kemp Travis for you. He only figures it as movin' it from one pocket to another."

"I refused both offers," Lisa said.

"Kemp Travis is a ketch," Hester said. "He's the kind that, sooner or later, seems to make money. He's better fixed than most right now."

"I have decided to go through with the agreement Frank O'Hara had made with you Barbees."

"You mean—go north with us as partners?" Hester almost screamed.

"There doesn't seem to be much choice if I'm to be a

ranch owner," Lisa said. "Abel says it's a losing proposition here."

"He's right," Hester said sorrowfully. "But movin' north won't be any picnic, let me tell you. Raisin' cattle's a hard way of makin' out at best, even durin' good times. An' who knows what'll happen to us in this new country. They tell me it gits so cold in winter up there your shadow freezes. It'll be a hard struggle, mark my word."

She gazed at Lisa. "Maybe you've made a mistake. Kemp will buy diamonds fer you some day, set you on a silk pillow."

"I sat on one once," Lisa said. "I thought it was wonderful. Now I never want it again, unless I can furnish it for myself."

"You can still change your mind," Hester declared. "Kemp'll ask ag'in. He's persistent, at least. Not that I'm pleadin' his case. Some day I'm afeared he's goin' to be a grief an' a calamity to me."

Lisa poured coffee. "Calamity? You mean—Abel?"

Hester sighed and nodded. "Abel has always believed Kemp could have warned us the time that bunch of Comanches jumped us. So does Paul Drexel. Sometimes I'm afeared Paul is goin' to pick a quarrel with Kemp an' have it out with guns."

"Paul? Paul Drexel?" Lisa was disbelieving.

"Yes, Paul. Don't be fooled by the way he's always laughin' an' friskin' around. Paul saw his own Paw an' Maw butchered right before his eyes when he was only twelve years old. He bears that debt ag'in Kemp."

"I don't understand."

"Paul lived with his folks five miles north o' here. They had settled there a couple o' years before. All that saved him was that he was out in the brush an' the Injuns didn't see him. They killed Alice an' George Drexel an' burned their cabin. Then they came on an' hit us here at Monte Vista. My own husband was killed in that fight. He got up from a sick bed to help stand 'em off."

"But what did Kemp Travis have to do——?"

"We learned later from a man who worked at Kemp's ranch that Kemp had sighted that war party early in the mornin', headin' toward the Drexel place an' Monte Vista. 'Stead o' warnin' George Drexel an' us, he rode to his own ranch an' barricaded. He let us fight it out alone. If it hadn't been that Monte Vista was 'dobe-built, we'd all have been wiped out."

"You really fear Abel or Paul Drexel will fight Kemp Travis because of that?" Lisa asked.

"So afeared of it I pray every night that the good Lord will keep 'em apart," Hester said. "An' Matthew, too."

"Matthew?"

"He saw his father killed. He's got no use for Kemp. They're all determined men. Kemp's got riders what are mean an' quarrelsome an' think nothin' of shootin' a human bein'. The worst of the lot is Coe Slade."

"Sam Miller mentioned that name," Lisa said.

"Kemp's a rough man himself," Hester said. "He'll never enter the pearly gates of heaven. He's a sharp man in any kind of a deal, cattle or buttons. He's had a good education, but he uses it only for his own gain."

"Speaking of education, why does Abel—why is it that Abel——?" Lisa found herself floundering.

Hester nodded sadly. "I know what you mean. Abel never had time for schoolin'. His father began ailin' when Abel was only a boy. Tom wasn't a well man for five or six years before his death. I had to depend on Abel. Schools were mighty scarce in these parts. What learnin' he got was what he picked up as best he could. After his Dad was gone he saw to it that Matthew had teachin'. An' Paul, too. Paul's been with us ever since his folks was taken. Abel sent both of 'em to boardin' school in Austin. We was makin' money in cattle then. Beef was bringin' good prices in Louisiana before the war. Abel was in the war for two years. He come home wounded, sick an' thin."

She looked proudly at Lisa. "Don't ever make any mistake about Abel," she said. "He's the most highly educated man you'll ever meet. Book learnin' ain't always education."

She was silent a moment. She gazed around. "You can't stay here, Elizabeth. You know that, 'specially after last night. We can watch over you better at Monte Vista."

Lisa finally arose. "I'll get my things packed," she said.

She left the bunkhouse and walked to the lean-to. She was busy there with her luggage when she heard a rider approaching at a fast gait. She hurried into the yard.

The arrival was Paul Drexel. "Where's Abel?" he shouted as he swung down. "Chepita told us at the ranch he might be here."

"He's brush poppin'!" Hester said. "Or with the herd. An' that's where you an' Matthew ought to be."

"Matt'll find him," Paul said. "He headed for the bedgrounds."

"Where were you and Matthew last night?" Hester demanded severely. "You never came home."

"In San Ysidro. We learned something that——"

"Drinkin' an' gamblin' ag'in," Hester interrupted scathingly. "Dancin' with that Spanish hussie at the Mud Turtle. That Dolores. High heels an' no stockin's. Oh, I know all about her an' you, Paul Drexel. An' Matthew's just as wild."

"You're giving us a mighty bad reputation with Elizabeth," Paul protested. "We've learned something important. And from Dolores."

"I don't want to hear anything from such a source," Hester stated, aquiver with righteousness.

"We found out why Kemp Travis is so bent on buying beef cattle."

Hester's head popped straighter. "You did? Why?"

"But you said you didn't want to listen to anything that came from Dolores, Aunt Hester."

"Never mind that, you grinnin' scamp. Don't keep me on pins."

"There are two strangers in town. One is a retired army officer named Major Gilchrist. The other is a younger man, Perry Diehl. Diehl's father is the principal owner of Diehl & Diehl, a big cattle outfit that operates in California and Nevada."

"I've heard of them," Hester nodded. "Who ain't?"

"Diehl & Diehl are in the market for six thousand head of beef cattle," Paul stated.

"Six thousand!" Hester exclaimed. "Good glory! What price are they offerin'?"

"They started out at twelve dollars a head. Kemp Travis has been dickering with them. He's been asking twenty-five. I understand they've gone up to seventeen and a half for beef delivered in good condition at Reno, Nevada, before winter."

"Seventeen an' a half? Son, you ain't been drinkin' too much ag'in, now have you?"

"Not a drop in hours, to my regret," Paul declared.

"You must have heard wrong. Why'd they pay that much?"

"Diehl & Diehl slaughters and dresses beef as well as raising it," Paul said. "They furnish meat to the mining towns in Nevada and the California mountains, and to San Francisco and other places. They haven't said so, of course, for they're out to buy at the best price possible, but it's already common knowledge in San Ysidro that Diehl & Diehl have been caught with their britches down."

"A scandalous thing to say in the presence of ladies," Hester remonstrated. "Watch your tongue, Paul."

"They've got contracts for meat that they can't fill," Paul explained. "They're in a tight fix."

Lisa spoke. "But why? I've heard that California is full of cattle. The Spanish ranchers . . ."

"Not any longer. They've had a bad drought for three years. California and Nevada are full of cattle, but the most of them are dead and skinned for their hides. They're already short of meat. By the middle of summer the price of beef is going to be sky-high out there."

"How'd these two men happen to come to San Ysidro?" Hester asked skeptically.

"They were in San Antonio first and heard that roundup was being run early by ranches in the San Ysidro and trail herds being put up, with prices at rock bottom. That was what they were looking for. We're far enough west so that we've got a week's advantage on herds from the ranges east of us. It's a long trail to Nevada. They want beef no later than September twentieth. It's said they'll pay a bonus for earlier delivery."

Paul added slowly. "Don't get the idea Diehl & Diehl are here to throw away money. It's eighteen hundred miles to this place, Reno. And across hard country."

Lisa spoke again. "Dolores seems to be quite a mine of information. Where did she learn all this?"

Paul grinned. "She has a wide circle of acquaintances. She dances and sips an occasional glass of sarsaparilla with riders from Kemp Travis's outfit, I'm sorry to say."

"Sa'sp'rilla, my foot!" Hester snorted. "She drinks hard likker like a fish."

"All the news didn't come from her," Paul explained. "San Ysidro is alive with gossip, and some of it seems to be hitting the mark. We clinched it by talking to Major Gilchrist and Perry Diehl themselves this morning."

"What did they say?" Hester exclaimed.

"They hadn't wanted to advertise their presence, or their need for cattle, but they know it's leaked out, and that they'll have to pay. So they did a little talking. Kemp was in San Antonio when they first showed up there. He did his best to keep them away from other cattlemen until he got their names on a contract to buy six thousand head of cattle. He brought them to his ranch and has been wining and dining them for three or four days."

"Ha!" Hester burst out. "Now we know why Kemp started tryin' to buy beef from us all of a sudden."

Paul nodded. "But Gilchrist and Diehl guessed that he couldn't supply that many beeves from his own outfit, and was stalling until he could buy cattle cheap from other owners—meaning us and Frank O'Hara. They thanked Kemp for entertaining them and moved to town. They're still buying three thousand head from Kemp, which is about all he can put on the trail in a hurry, but they figured they'd prefer to make their own deals for the rest. They talked to Frank O'Hara."

Lisa spoke quickly. "When?"

"The morning before Frank was shot," Paul said. "They went to O'Hara House, but Frank was drunk and ugly. He was making threats against Abel. They went back to town, deciding to wait until Frank had sobered up before making any further move."

"What did you tell 'em about us?" Hester asked.

"Matt told them we're about ninety per cent rounded up and road-branded, and could put nearly two thousand head on the trail in a hurry."

"Three thousand or better," Hester said. "Lisa is throwin' Triangle O in with Bar B."

Paul uttered a delighted whoop and threw his arms around Lisa. She found herself lifted off the ground and whirled. He kissed her lustily and set her down, grinning.

"Stop that!" Hester commanded. "When can Abel talk to these men?"

"Matt invited them to Monte Vista for supper tonight."

"Tonight? Oh, my land! Oh, misery! Ain't that just like a man?"

Abel arrived at Monte Vista as Hester and her helpers were starting their frenzied activities. He came at once to speak to Lisa.

"So you've decided to throw in with us?" he asked.

"Yes." She let that statement stand on its own merits.

Hester spoke. "How long will it take to git to this place in Nevada, Abel?"

"It's four months' drive, at best," he said. "It's a good month's drive beyond the farthest big river, which is the Rio Colorado of the west."

There was a hollow sound in Hester's voice. "It's acrost the 'Pache country, then."

"Wouldn't it be easier to drive north to the Union Pacific Railroad and ship the cattle?" Lisa asked.

"Too far to the railroad an' too far to ship after you get there," Abel said. "The railroad crosses deserts, too. We'd lose the biggest part of 'em, crowded into cars for thet long a spell. Shippin' costs would eat up all the earnin', even if we got through with 'em. The only profit in Longhorns is thet they carry theirselves to market on their own laigs. They'll thrive in country where other breed would lean down."

He saw that she had more questions ready. "There's plenty o' unsold Texas cattle in Kansas," he continued. "Wintered there. Some will head west when the owners hear there's a market. They'll have a hard trail by way of the old California road. Mud, rain an' high rivers 'til the weather clears in June. It's always thet way on the north plains, they say. They won't be within even shippin' distance o' Reno 'til late fall. Then prices will drop. But Diehl & Diehl need beef before thet. It's my guess they figure about six thousand head will tide 'em over."

"Where did you learn all this?" Lisa asked.

"Cattle an' trails are my business. We're in the right spot to cash in on this, because we've got a beef herd about ready an' have got the advantage in distance an' weather. We kin make it by way of a trail called Beale's Road through the middle of Arizona Territory. That part of it'll be cooler an' shorter than the Gila River trail to the south. But there's no avoidin' the desert beyond."

"Abel, you ride into town an' get barbered an' a haircut," Hester commanded. "You could do with a new necktie too, if there's one to be had at the store."

CHAPTER 11

Lisa gazed at herself by lamplight in the mirror in her room at Monte Vista. She wore an evening gown, her only one, which Hester had pounced on with a cry of triumph when her trunk had been opened.

She turned, marking the good lines of her figure. Slender, but with the curving allure that was necessary for a glove-fitting affair such as this. It was an emerald-hued gown that she had last worn to the theater in the opulent era. She had managed to cling to this gown through the barren days.

Her shoulders were bare and there was revealing, yet concealing, amount of bosom visible. She looked at Hester. She saw in Hester a wistful envy—almost a resentment. That reassured her, told her that all was right and that she was what she had intended to be—desirable, very feminine.

"Blast you," Hester said. "I've always wanted to look like that. Pure, but just a little wanton. Temptin' to all men. It'll likely be writ ag'in the both of us in the Good Book. It'll be held ag'in us when the reckonin' comes. We're tryin' to sway men by worldly wiles."

"You may be right," Lisa said.

The rumble of men's voices drifted from the main room. Lisa had heard the guests arrive by carriage some thirty minutes earlier.

"I'm ready to put my figure on exhibition for the sake of selling cattle," she said.

"Don't talk like that," Hester groaned.

Hester, for all her feverish activity during the day, had found time to array herself in a prim, blue dress that was becoming.

Lisa took Hester's arm, gathered the train of her dress and they entered the main room. Matthew and the two visitors were present, and also Paul Drexel, but Abel was not in sight.

All of the men gazed. Lisa enjoyed that moment. Matthew came hurrying and led them to the introductions. "Miss Randolph," he said, "is our new associate in the cattle business."

Major Gilchrist was a graying ramrod of a man, distin-

guished of manner and dress and precise of speech. Perry
Diehl, vigorous, alert, with frank brown eyes, seemed to be
in his early thirties.

Gilchrist bowed low to Hester. With courtly privilege, he
held Lisa's hand for a time in both his own, gazing at her.
"I must say I did not expect to meet such attractive ladies.
I have heard much about you, Mrs. Barbee. And you, Miss
Randolph, of course are the young lady who inherited the
ranch known as Triangle O. Matthew has told us about it."

It developed that Lisa and the Major and Perry Diehl
had mutual friends in Chicago and also in St. Louis, where
Lisa had often visited. They talked. They laughed. The terrors
of the past few days were erased for a time from her immediate thoughts. For the moment she was back to the era of the
golden spoon—easy conversation, modulated voices, polished diction.

Paul took part in some of the exchange and the banter,
and was perfectly at ease. Matthew remained in the background, smiling remotely at the right times and in the right
moments, listening with only half attention. Matthew, Lisa
realized, was treading the golden clouds. He had a way of
retreating into his own world when the matter under discussion did not interest him.

She saw him turn, saw a warm and welcoming light come to
life within him. Abel had entered the room. Lisa was struck by
the realization that Matthew had a close spiritual tie with
the uncultured, practical-mannered brother. She recalled the
way Abel had halted to take in the beauty of the sunrise at
Triangle O, and she knew now that she had been seeing in
him the same flight of poetic fancy that made the world
something different to Matthew than to other people.

"Sorry I'm late, gentlemen," Abel said.

He came into the better glow of the lamplight. Hester
uttered a small, startled sound. There was nothing poetic
about Abel's present aspect. His right eye was swollen and
turning purple. Another bruise glowed lividly on his cheek-
bone. A strip of medical plaster adorned his chin. His garb
bore the stain of inground dust, despite much brushing. His
white shirt had suffered damage, his string tie was still slightly
off center.

He walked closer. "You're Major Gilchrist, I reckon," he
said, extending his left hand. "Excuse me fer not offerin' the
proper hand. My right one ain't exactly in workin' order. An'
you, sir, must be Mr. Perry Diehl. Welcome to Monte Vista."

Hester stepped forward and straightened his tie. "This,"
she said proudly, "is my eldest son. This is Abel."

The visitors accepted Abel's handshake and glanced around to see if this was some sort of a joke.

Abel offered no further explanation. He moved to the table, poured drinks for the men and handed them their glasses. He lifted his own. "Your health, Major," he said. "An' yours, Mr. Diehl."

They drank. The ease was gone. There was a smolder in Abel's dark eyes. Lisa felt tension building up in her. She was aware that his gaze was upon her, and with great disapproval.

Major Gilchrist cleared his throat twice, started to say something, then gave it up. Perry Diehl was frowning, pondering whether to be amused or offended. It was obvious they were not only puzzled by Abel's appearance but by his rough manner of speech, in contrast to that of his more cultured brother.

Lisa saw Matthew straighten. His attitude of polite remoteness vanished. Apprehension drove through her. She saw that in Matthew was a great pride in his brother and a readiness to resent any affront to him. Paul Drexel had stiffened also. The bond of affection included him. The three men stood shoulder to shoulder, as they had at the inquest.

Lisa stepped into the breach. She moved forward and looked at Abel. "You've been fighting. Who?"

"It don't matter," he said briefly.

"How'd the other fellow look?" Perry Diehl asked, trying to make conversation. It was a time-worn attempt at humor and he realized it. He flushed and fell silent.

"It's time we went in to supper," Hester spoke hastily.

Lisa accepted Major Gilchrist's arm, and they followed Hester and Perry Diehl. Hester and Chepita had done themselves proud. The table was crisp with white linen and shining with silver from Hester's cherished belongings which had been hastily unpacked. Crystal wine glasses stood ready.

It was a picture of refinement. But the informality that had fled at Abel's appearance could not be recalled. It was an awkward meal of long silences and forced talk. Abel spoke of the weather and inquired into the state of the guests' health. He was solicitous in regard to the hardships they might have suffered on their journey.

And more and more keenly Lisa became sure that he was frowning on her presence at the table.

She had noted lately that he had improved in both his grammar and diction, but now it seemed to her that he had decided to turn back.

Matthew sat silent, watching Abel. In him, Lisa saw, was

an inner grief for his brother and an agony of self-reproach. Hester was the most silent of all. She sat, pretending to eat, but Lisa noticed that she had not really touched a morsel. In Paul Drexel's handsome face was deep regret.

Lisa went a little limp when the coffee cups were finally pushed back. The ordeal was about over. Major Gilchrist seemed happy to find a chance to bring up the purpose of their visit.

"Now," Gilchrist said. "As you know, we are in the market for beef cattle to be delivered to Diehl & Diehl in September at Reno, Nevada. Steers, of course, but some barren cows are acceptable. The stock must arrive in condition to fatten and finish off on good grass in short order and——"

Abel got to his feet, interrupting the Major. "Sorry, gentlemen," he said. "We've got no cattle fer sale."

"What?" Lisa exclaimed. She arose and looked from face to face. She saw the determination in Abel. Matthew was smiling again——smiling at all the inconsistencies and vagaries of human nature. Hester's head was bowed.

Lisa stood straighter and straighter. All the color fled from her. "What Mr. Barbee means," she said, "is that he doesn't believe in putting a woman on display as a means of tempting you men into a business deal."

She turned and walked to the door. "And I agree with him," she said. "It was my fault. I'm sorry. I was the one responsible for it."

She walked out and closed the door back of her. The only sound was the steady refrain her high heels aroused on the gallery as she walked to her room. There, back of her closed door, she stood for a time gazing again into the mirror.

It was some time before she heard the supper party break up. She was still sitting at the dressing table. The guests left, heading for San Ysidro in a buggy. She continued to gaze into the mirror, seeing her image and yet not seeing it. She was trying to look beyond it into the future. She was thinking that this future held nothing for her. She seemed to have reached another dead end.

A hand tapped the door. The voice that answered in response to her question was Abel's.

"In a moment," she responded. She pulled on a dress and opened the door.

He was bareheaded. His damaged eye had turned a deeper shade of purple. "You've got an apology comin'," he said.

"None is needed," she answered. "You were quite right. I'm sorry I spoiled the chance to sell the cattle."

She started to close the door, but he halted her. "Gilchrist an' Diehl are comin' back in the mornin' to take a look at the herd an' bring a contract."

"But I thought——!" she began.

"No less'n twenty-five hundred head, an' no more'n three thousand, to be delivered at a designated point within twenty miles of Reno, Nevada, by September twentieth."

"I don't understand——"

"You didn't spoil anything," he said. "They still need beef. An' they didn't seem to think they was bein' tempted. Fact is, they said the way you walked out o' thet room sort of decided 'em. They allowed thet they figured they was dealin' with a person who'd give them an honest shake."

"Where did you get that black eye?" she demanded.

"Twenty dollars a head, an' two bits a head bonus for every day we beat the contract date, provided the stock tallies out in good condition. No stags, no runts, no twisthorns."

There was a twinkle in his eye. "I keep forgittin' thet you don't savvy cattle. A twisthorn is an old steer thet——"

"There's a lot I don't savvy," she broke in. "Who did you fight with this time?"

"They'll sign the contract, provided you're still of a mind to throw in with us," he said.

"Of course I am. Now about this fighting——"

"I aim to have the herd on the trail in a week or less. We'll start roundin' up Triangle O territory tomorrow. I'll hire more extra riders an' run a fast gather."

He started to leave. Lisa spoke. "I'm happy you prevailed on those men to buy the cattle."

He paused. " 'Twasn't my doin'. You was the one."

Lisa smiled wanly. "Hardly. I shudder to think what their opinion of me might be."

He glared at her. For the first time she realized he had been drinking. "There wasn't ever any doubt in their minds about what you were," he said harshly. "A lady. With breedin'. An' there never was any doubt either about what they thought about me."

He turned and strode away down the gallery. It came to Lisa that he had reached some crossroads in his life. She started to withdraw into her room. Instead she stepped out, closed the door and followed him, staying at a distance.

Micah Jones, being a person of some privilege, occupied a small room at the south end of the addition to the main house. A light still burned there. She heard Abel knock sharply on the door. She moved nearer, passing the dogtrot and taking shelter back of one of the heavy posts that supported the gallery roof, shamelessly eavesdropping.

Micah opened the door. He evidently had been in his bunk,

reading. He held a dog-eared gazette in his hand, and was in his underwear.

Abel stalked past him into the room. "Git out the school books, Micah," he snapped.

"What?"

"I'm a-goin' to la'rn—learn—to talk right an' to read an' write better," Abel said. "Let's git busy."

"Holy, boiling sassafras, Abel! Are you drunk? It's the middle of the night."

"I'm ta'red of bein' looked down on," Abel said. " 'Specially by that no'thern woman. Git out the books. I got no time to waste. Both of us have got to be poppin' brush by daybreak. We're goin' to make the beef cut from Triangle O."

The door closed. Lisa listened to their voices in dispute. These sounds finally settled down to an occasional comment. Abel Barbee had started his formal education.

She turned, sensing that someone had come up silently in the ranch yard nearby. A man was standing in the darkness a few yards away. The moon had not yet arisen. Someone opened the bunkhouse door at a distance, and from this issued a beam of light. Against this she made out, vaguely, heavy, bronzed features and a powerful frame.

At that moment Hester called from the main house, "Elizabeth! 'Lizabeth! Where are you?"

The man walked away toward the bunkhouse. She felt that she had seen him somewhere before. That was easy to explain, of course. He must be a member of the roundup crew, and had every right to be crossing the yard at that moment. The bunkhouse door closed again.

Berating herself for too vivid an imagination, Lisa hurried to the main house.

Hester was waiting on the gallery. Lisa spoke first. "Who did Abel fight with today, Hester?" she demanded.

Hester did not answer. "Tell me!" Lisa insisted.

"Kemp Travis," Hester said reluctantly. "They fought with fists. It happened in town. People separated them an' tried to get them to shake hands. But they wouldn't."

Hester's voice was tired, heavy. "It was the mercy of the Lord thet neither of them happened to be armed. Abel was gettin' the best of it before the fight was stopped. But Kemp won't let it rest there, 'specially when he hears we've got half of the beef contract."

"What was it they fought about?" Lisa asked.

"It's been brewin', like I told you," Hester said.

"But something must have started it."

Hester said, "Good night, Elizabeth. You can sleep

sound. Paul an' Matthew will bed down outside your room ag'in tonight."

Lisa was sure then that somehow she was involved in the fight between Abel and Kemp Travis.

She placed the pistol within reach when she got into bed. She was comforted by the knowledge that Paul and Matthew were sleeping on guard at her door and window.

She lay awake. The ranch was sleeping, except for the occasional drift of muted voices. These came from Micah's quarters. It must have been well past midnight when these sounds ended. She heard a door open, heard Micah say wearily, "You're a real stubborn cuss, Abel."

Abel's footsteps receded toward the corral. She presently heard him ride away. His first session in book learning was ended, and he was now going out to see that all was well with the cattle. She wondered when he rested.

She dropped off into sound sleep herself. She slept all through the night.

CHAPTER 12

Lisa sat, sorting her personal belongings. She was storing in mothballs the greater part of the wardrobe she had brought to Texas. She sighed as she laid aside the majority of the finery. She retained only a minimum of practical attire, mainly cotton garments and stout footwear, some of which she had bought at the mercantile in San Ysidro.

It was early nightfall. She had been at Monte Vista for nearly a week . . . a week of unceasing activity. The contract with Diehl & Diehl had been signed, and the herd was assembled. It had been grazed westward a few miles each day and was now bedded some ten miles away.

A rider arrived and dismounted at the house. He came walking onto the gallery. She had learned to recognize the crisp sound of Abel's step.

She knew why he was here. She braced herself, aware that she was in for a scene with him. She arose, glanced into the mirror and started to smooth her hair. With a grimace, she decided against it. She even defiantly blew a loose strand out of her eyes and let it settle where it willed.

There had been considerable change in plans since the windfall of the beef contract had come along. Delivery of the herd to Diehl & Diehl was the immediate necessity. Complete removal of all stock to northern range would go over until the following year.

"We'll leave Mario Rojas in charge here," Abel had said. "He can hire what help he needs. We'll come back next year an' clean up, an' move what she-stuff an' breeders we want to where we settle."

The chuckwagon had joined the herd. The cookhouse was vacant and so was the bunkhouse. Because of the distance and the lack of supply points along the route, Abel had decided to add a second wagon to share the load.

The final tally showed three thousand and fifty-two head of Longhorns in the drive. "Seventeen hundred an' five are Bar B cattle, the rest from T O," Abel had informed Lisa.

Roundup of the Triangle O contribution had been accomplished speedily, with the help of nearly a score of riders from the vicinity whom Abel had hired for a few days' work.

However, joining the drive itself was another matter. Abel had intended to start out with a crew of fourteen, including a cook, a swamper and a horse wrangler. But he was still short-handed.

Lisa had taken it for granted, at first, that this was because the men were reluctant to face the hardships of so long a journey. But she had come to realize that the real reason was that there was general belief that their drive would never reach its destination. This view was based on something more definite than fear of the possible hazards of the trail.

The real reason became plain enough. The fist fight between Abel and Kemp Travis had brought into the open the growing feud. Travis had contracted for the other three thousand head that Diehl & Diehl needed, but to fill out that number he had been forced to buy some three hundred steers from small ranchers to the east. They had forced him to pay fifteen dollars a head, knowing that he could not afford to quibble. Travis would be heading west with his herd at about the same time as the departure of their B–T drive.

Micah Jones had signed up as a rider in the emergency. The cook was Nephi Smith, the jovial Negro with the melodious voice. Ygnacio Valdez, a long-time rider for Bar B, was with the drive. A shy young beanpole from the Tennessee hills, answering to only the name of Shadrack, was horse wrangler. Tom Zook, a seamy, sun-dried man who had to knead his knee joints into submission each morning, was to act as cook's swamper and driver of the hoodlum wagon. A talkative rider named Al Quirk had been taken on by Abel for want of better material. Lon Melton, a blocky, freckled young Texan, was another member of ' the crew.

"Looks like we'll pull out two, three men shy, Miss 'Lizabeth," Nephi Smith had said. "But we got Matt Barbee an' Paul Drexel, don't forgit. They's young an' tough an' kin ride anythin' with four laigs. An' Massa Abel! He's as good as half a crew all by hisself."

Now the footsteps of this man who was as good as half a crew were at her door. She heard Hester join him.

His hand tapped the portal. Lisa opened it and said, "Come in!"

Abel entered, removing his dusty hat. Hester followed, looking apprehensive. Lisa had been storing her unneeded possessions in the big trunk. The remainder were being packed in a small trunk of tough leather which she had bought in San Ysidro on Hester's advice.

Abel frowningly eyed this division of her wardrobe. "Hester tells me you ain't—aren't goin' back to Chicago."

"No," Lisa said. "I'm going with the herd. I've given Sam Miller power of attorney to act for me here. There seems to be nothing, really, for me to stay for."

"It's out o' the question, o' course," he stated grimly.

"Why? Hester's going."

"Thet's different. An' she's only along to drive the hoodlum wagon 'til we hire another man. Tom Zook can make out as a rider for awhile. Then he'll go back to drivin' an' helpin' the cook."

"Why is it different?" Lisa challenged.

Abel glared at her. "Hester's been on trails. She knows cattle, an' she's been around cowboys. She'll be of some help. She kin drive a wagon, an'——"

"I can learn. I'm going along."

Abel turned to his mother. "Talk to her, Hester."

Hester patted Lisa on the shoulder. "You don't exactly understand, Elizabeth. Women like you jest don't travel with trail herds. I warned you Abel wouldn't approve."

"You're a woman," Lisa said.

"You'd cause us a hell of a lot of trouble," Abel snapped.

"In what way?" Lisa inquired grimly.

"Why—why—a lot o' ways." He was floundering.

Hester spoke. "There're problems, dear. Why, sometimes fer days there ain't even a bush big enough to hide behind fer privacy."

"You seem to think you will make out," Lisa said. "I will also."

"You kin git to Reno easier an' safer by goin' back the way you came an' takin' the railroad west," Abel said. "You'll git there a lot faster, too."

Lisa shook her head. "You're still short of riders, even with Tom Zook working with the herd. Well, Nephi Smith tells me he's a cowhand first and a cook afterwards. I asked Micah, and he said Nephi is a top hand. He'd prefer to ride rather than cook. Hester and I will take over both the cooking and the wagons. That will give you Nephi."

She eyed him levelly. "And don't try to scare me with any more talk about bushes and privacy," she added.

"This won't be like joggin' a pony cart over a street in Chicago," he said. "You'll be drivin' four hard-jawed mules. An' a wagon thet weighs up to a ton an' a half loaded."

"I've about finished packing," she said. "I will leave what I don't need here to be brought on next year."

"The mules," said Abel helplessly, "won't be the only knotheaded critters around thet there wagon."

"The word 'there' is superfluous," Lisa said calmly. "The word that you call 'thet' is correctly pronounced as 'that.'"

He towered over her, wrath blazing in him. "You don't know what the trail's like. Don't start." Then he stalked out.

Hester gazed wide-eyed. "You almost drove him to layin' a hand on you, Elizabeth. You hurt his pride. That's hard for a man like Abel to bear."

"I learned what brought on the fistfight between him and Kemp Travis," Lisa said.

Hester looked wry. "Who told you?"

"Chepita. It seems that Kemp Travis referred to me as a fallen woman. He used a stronger name for it which Chepita was too modest to repeat. Abel called him a liar."

"I ought to take a stick to Chepita," Hester said. She added heavily, "I only pray that they stay away from each other from now on. But they won't."

Hester looked around. "If you're really determined to go, I reckon nothin' I say will stop you. Better hustle your packin'. The wagon'll be here in an hour to take us out to the wagons."

Lisa was startled. "In an hour? Tonight?"

Hester nodded. "This very night. Abel's startin' the drive in the mornin'. There's breakfast to be ready for the crew at daybreak an' camp chores to finish while the herd is trailin' out. Tomorrow the cattle head west for keeps. An' no delay."

Lisa looked around helplessly. "Why—why, I thought there'd be a little more time to——" She paused and gazed at Hester, then said, "I'll be ready in thirty minutes."

In little more than that time Micah Jones drove a light wagon up to the house and called, "All ready, ladies."

He lashed their scant luggage to the deck and helped them to the seat where he joined them. The team snatched the wagon out of its tracks and they were on their way. Lisa looked back as the vehicle swung past the corral and out into the open blaze of the starlight.

Monte Vista was a dark, fading bulk in the night. The pattern of the roofs and chimneys stood out for a moment against the stars, and then was lost in the darkness behind them.

Hester did not look back or utter a sound. There was in her a wordless resignation to this parting from all the scenes and memories of the golden days of her life.

I'll never be a stoic like that, Lisa thought. *I'll never be able to keep my grief bottled up.*

The wheels leaped high over ruts and rocks, coming down with crashings that jarred the passengers to the teeth. The horses never slowed their rushing pace.

A particularly vicious jolt nearly tossed Hester from the

seat. She straightened her bonnet. "An' this is only the beginnin'," she said. "We've got eighteen hundred miles o' this ahead of us."

Presently, on the wind, Lisa became aware of the wild animal presence, peculiar to Longhorns. It dominated the night and yet was a part of its wild loneliness. The team slowed and became subdued.

"We're nearing the herd," Micah spoke. He also was quiet. A medley of respect and antagonism came into his voice. "The double-blasted, damned herd. We'll have that smell in our noses, in our hair, in our souls until we hate it and hate them. We'll hate each other, too."

The outline of the chuckwagon loomed in the mellow glow of the fire. Lisa made out the forms of men sleeping, wrapped in quilts. Abel and Matthew were still awake and came to the wagon to meet them.

Far out in the darkness Lisa heard a deep and heavy stirring. A steer began bawling. Others took it up.

Abel and Matthew stood taut and listening. The sleepers awakened but did not move. They lay waiting. Men on duty with the herd were singing in a chanting monotone, the sound frail and thin in the night.

Slowly the movement faded and the bawling died out. The singing ended. Silence came again.

"All right," Abel said. "Seems like they've settled down."

He helped Lisa to the ground.

CHAPTER 13

Lisa awakened when Ygnacio Valdez, who was on the last night trick with the herd, rode to the wagons, kicked the embers of the previous night's fire into life, added fresh fuel and scratched his fingernails on the canvas of their sleeping quarters to make sure she and Hester were aroused.

Feeble dawn was outlining the weather seams in the hood of the hoodlum wagon in which they slept. Lisa lay a moment, misering the warmth of the blankets, then dressed in haste, her teeth chattering. Later on the day would be hot, no doubt, but the bleak hour before sunrise always held this thin and dispiriting chill.

She and Hester emerged and began preparing breakfast. The crew awakened. Shadrack brought the remuda with a thud of hooves into a rope corral beyond the wagons, the bells on the two mares clanging. Flapjacks and hot coffee were wolfed down.

Mounts were roped from among the milling animals in the rope barrier. There was the usual wild moment of pitching and sunfishing on the part of the horses and yelling on the part of the riders. Then they were gone, hurrying to where the herd was grazing in the pink light of dawn.

Soon the cattle were all in motion, their bawling a sustained chorus, punctuated by the popping of rope ends and shouting.

Before the sun peered over the rim of a vast and vacant land, the Longhorns were strung out and moving steadily westward. The dust began to rise.

Another day had started in a routine that was to grow very familiar to Lisa. Abel returned to the wagons. Lisa and Hester, along with Nephi, whose duty it was to help with these tasks, had the cooking gear and bedrolls loaded and the mules hooked up.

Abel spoke to Lisa as she prepared to climb to the seat of the supply wagon. "We'll be crossin' the Pecos the day after tomorrow. We'll come on a stage trail from El Paso. You likely can get passage no'th, if the line's still operatin'. You might have to wait a day or two 'til it comes along."

Lisa made no comment. She mounted to the seat and adjusted the reins.

"Beyond the river we go deeper into the country," he went on. "There won't be any chance o' turnin' back or ketchin' a stage 'til we hit the Rio Grande quite a piece west."

When Lisa still did not speak he removed his hat and mopped his forehead with his neckerchief. "Still headstrong, ain't you?"

Lisa released the brake. "Yes."

"Keep close up," he said abruptly. "Stay near Hester."

Abel rode to the rear of the wagon, lifted the flap and peered in. He pulled the bedrolls aside and found a six-shooter which had been placed there in its holster and wrapped in the belt.

"Whose gun?" he asked.

Lisa gave him a look. "It's going to be hot today," she said.

He smiled thinly. "At least you're not a squealer. It's Al Quirk's. He's a damned fool."

Accompanied by Nephi, he rode away toward the drive, carrying the offending weapon. He had brought along a supply of pistols and rifles, as well as considerable ammunition. He saw to it that every man was supplied with arms, and had given strict orders that every member of the crew carry at least a six-shooter whenever he was with the herd or apart from the wagons for any cause.

"Any man who forgets will be given his pay an' set afoot, no matter where we are," he had said.

Lisa had learned that this command included herself and Hester. Both of them had been given a dressing down for failing to take pistols with them when they had been apart from the wagons for only a short time a few evenings earlier.

The pistols were cumbersome affairs, in Lisa's viewpoint. Nearly all of the collection were of the cap and ball variety although, like the one Abel had given her, there were a few that had been converted to cartridge loading. Even the easygoing Micah Jones was not reconciled to the necessity of lugging more than six pounds of metal in addition to a bull-hide holster and a belt, hour after hour, day after day, in the blazing sun.

Al Quirk, the loquacious one, was particularly opposed to such effort. "Ain't been a Comanche this far off the Llano Estacado in two years," Quirk had grumbled. "Anyway, what's the sense of it here where you kin see an Injun an hour before he could git within shootin' distance?"

"There's more'n one use for a pistol," Abel had said. "I found a friend o' mine once, who'd broke both laigs when his horse threw him while he was brush poppin'. There was javalinas around. If he'd have been carryin' his gun he could have fetched me, for I wasn't too fur away. But the wild pigs found him first—while he was still alive by the looks. An' there're other reasons why you might need to do some shootin'. One you know about."

Even so, Lisa believed that Abel's discipline was too rigid. She had said as much to Paul Drexel one evening.

Paul had shrugged. "Out here it isn't just one man looking out for himself alone. We've got to hang together. You can't have anyone falling into the drag like some of the cattle do. Abel's carrying a lot of worry. A dozen lives to think about. And, of course, the herd. Three thousand flitterears."

"I'm sure it's the cattle that come first," she had commented.

Paul had eyed her. "You don't know Abel, do you? You haven't come to know him at all."

Lisa was thinking of what Paul had said as she drove along. And she fell to wondering again what Abel had meant when he had told Quirk that one of the reasons for always carrying a weapon was "one that you know about."

The chuckwagon, with Hester driving, had taken the lead as usual. Both vehicles were lurching over the bunchgrass, gradually pulling abreast of the herd.

At noon the wagons made a short stop and Lisa and Hester furnished a quick meal to the riders. The march resumed.

Afternoon turned hot and drowsy and Lisa fell to daydreaming. It was the first time she had indulged in that luxury in months.

She felt utterly at peace. The creak and complaint of the wheels, the grind of the rims through the loose soil, the ceaseless bobbing of the four pairs of long ears ahead—all these merged into a familiar performance that lulled her.

Monte Vista and the ruins of O'Hara House were nearly three hundred miles astern now. She was appalled to realize that she was viewing them as something remembered in a past that was fading into the mists. Only the recollection of Frank O'Hara looking at her with that wonder in his eyes, and the poignant sadness of his death, were vivid with her.

Even the attempts on her life were events that seemed to have happened to another person. It was a mysterious episode that time and distance was dimming in her mind.

Little else existed now except the wagons, the sky and

the land and the herd. This was their universe. The herd was the sun around which they revolved.

"Damn the cattle!" Lisa said aloud. She spoke it without rancor, almost with affection.

She glimpsed the herd occasionally whenever the wagon crested a swell in the immense plain over which they were crawling. It was a lengthy, serpentine blemish on the surface of the land slightly west and south of her, half a mile away.

In the clear air, she could make out the riders—point and swing. The men who were working drag were hidden in the thick dust that was blowing in the hot afternoon wind. Lisa had learned that the progress of the herd was no faster than that made by the slowest cattle in the drag.

Abel was there somewhere in the dust, pushing the laggards. He usually was. Paul, the dashing and natty one, was riding point, guiding the way, along with the faster-walking and belligerent steers that were the natural leaders of the herd. Matthew rode swing, dreaming his dreams and letting the slow miles and the slow days drift over him. But Abel was the one who was always driving the cattle—driving the men.

Far astern were places bearing names Lisa had never before heard. The Nueces, the dry fork of Devil's River, the Concho; watercourses, or where watercourses should have been, for some had been arid. These were the landmarks of this region.

They had been traveling across the face of a great tableland for the past week. Dry and endless, it gave support mainly to the bunchy plains grass and stunted mesquite. When the herd had first moved into this vastness Lisa had watched a line of purple mountains in the distance and had taken it for granted that they would make their night's camp near them. After a week, those mountains were receding below the horizon to the southwest. New shadows were rising ahead of them, for they were following a northeasterly direction.

The riders were now talking about Horsehead Crossing, a ford across the Pecos River. She was aware that tension was building up among them as they drew nearer this place, day by day.

Hester had heard of Horsehead Crossing. "They say the trail to it is marked by the skulls of dead horses an' cattle an' dead men," she had told Lisa. "It's been used since the early Spanish times. It's a thirsty drive from the Concho to the Pecos in summer, but we're lucky in startin' early. There's been rain this spring an' the *charcos*—thet means ponds or low places—are full, an' we've got no water problem."

Hester had added in that heavy voice that was her landmark of worry, "At least right now."

The men feared this fording of the river, but none voiced their apprehension openly. Pride forbade that. Hester feared the crossing also. Lisa had never seen the fording of a big river. She was afraid only of this enormous, impersonal ocean of land through which they moved without apparent progress. She understood now what Abel's threat to set a man afoot really meant.

But it was more pleasant to forget these things for the moment and let her thoughts drift along as aimlessly as those fleecy clouds sailed overhead on their flat hulls. To let life move at the unhurried pace of the cattle.

Somewhere ahead was Hester and the chuckwagon. Somewhere to the west was the herd. Both were hidden now, for Lisa was traveling through another of the series of rolling, grassy swells. Each knoll and swale ahead looked exactly like the ones astern.

She felt completely alone and content. She thought of Chicago and the life she had once known. She tried to recall friends, old beaux, acquaintances. These memories seemed clear enough—and yet the faces she sought to visualize would not quite come into focus.

She found her reflections centering more clearly upon Abel and his problems. The peace of the day was troubled. Abel always seemed to arouse within her a clash of emotion.

He sat with Micah Jones each night apart from the others, poring over textbooks by the light of an oil lantern. He carried books with him while with the herd, and she had seen him reading as he rode along at times when the Longhorns were tractable, seen his lips moving as he memorized passages.

And then there was Paul, who pursued her with his assured and sensual courtship. And Matthew, whose gaze she found often upon her, longing and hopeful.

These and other fancies held her as the slow miles passed. She came back to reality at last and looked around. How long she had been out of sight of the herd and chuckwagon she could not estimate. The sun seemed to be in the wrong position and was startlingly low on the horizon.

Lisa came to her feet, gazing around. She surprised the mules by snapping the whip.

She decided that the run of the swells had caused the mules to drift eastward. She swung them around. They opposed her, balking and shaking their heads, but she let them feel the flick of the whip, and they broke into a gallop that was so wild and unexpected it almost unseated her.

She brought them under control, and hoped the wagon had suffered no damage, for it had bounced heavily over hummocks and small rain gullies.

She headed the team to a rise. From the crest she gazed, expecting to sight either the herd or the other wagon. All that she saw was empty country. Directly ahead was rougher terrain than she had seen in this region. A badlands of eroded ravines and clay buttes barred the way in that direction.

She pulled the mules to a halt. She found herself breathing fast. She peered around wildly. She decided that she had been wrong and the mules had been right. She swung the wagon in the opposite path, giving them their heads. She had heard that animals would, by instinct, find their way back to their companions.

The mules trotted along steadily, but after a time it seemed to Lisa they were moving into the rough country she had been trying to avoid. A deep ravine loomed ahead. She realized that the mules were following a path of least effort downhill into the badlands.

She now fought panic. Something cold and terrifying entered her mind. She managed to turn the wagon, but it was touch and go for a moment against capsizing as it hung askew on the slant. Finally it straightened.

She tried to backtrack, following the wagon's own wheelmarks. Surely this would carry her back to the level plain itself—back to where they had wandered into this maze.

The wheeltracks faded on a stretch of hardpan which she had not remembered passing over. She had a choice of half a dozen gloomy swales as her probable route.

These were gloomy because the sun had gone down. She could not believe she had been lost this long. She remembered that these plains were said to be the route the tribes followed on their raids against the settlements. She reached beneath the seat and found the pistol Abel had given her. She held it in her lap.

The mules were tiring, and she realized she had been pushing them hard. She let them rest, forcing herself to sit quietly until they had stopped blowing. That time of inaction was torture. Panicky impulse urged her to leave these stolid animals and race on foot somewhere—anywhere.

She resisted that. She thought of firing signal shots but ruled against that also, fearing that gunfire might bring Indians.

The mules moved ahead again, mounting a hogback. Higher, higher. From its crest she saw the rim of the plains. As soon as they topped this summit she found herself gazing at a great sweep of open country.

She uttered a cry of joy. Ahead, only a mile or so, she made out the great shadow of a grazing herd of cattle. Not far from it was a wagon camp, with a fire offering a small red beacon in the growing twilight.

She shed a tear or two. She found herself utterly spent. Thankful to the depths of her heart, she put the mules to a weary trot. She replaced the pistol in its holster beneath the seat.

She suddenly arose to her feet, gripping the bow for support. She stared, puzzled. A mile or more north of the camp, she made out another ragged dark shadow spread across the plain. More cattle! A second herd!

There were two wagons in the camp toward which she was heading. This was not her own outfit.

Her approach had been sighted. Two riders came out from the camp to meet her. Dusk was deepening swiftly. Semidarkness came before they met. The wagon fire was still some distance away.

It was not until they were close at hand that she recognized Kemp Travis in his dusty trail garb. Travis's companion remained in the background and evidently was a trail hand. He was unshaven, his face almost hidden by the shadows beneath his weathered hat.

Travis pulled up alongside the wagon, peering. "Well! Well! Elizabeth! The lady who joined as partner with the man who murdered her prospective husband. The heiress who lost no time trying to make a profit out of the O'Hara estate."

CHAPTER *14*

Travis was smiling, but there was a festering rancor in him, the bitterness of a domineering man whose plans had been broken and whose offer of marriage had been rejected.

"I thought this was our drive," Lisa said. "I'm lost."

"Does it make any difference?" Travis asked silkily.

"What do you mean?" Lisa demanded.

"The thought occurs to me that, sooner or later, you'll tire of Abel Barbee's righteousness. Perhaps you already have."

Lisa started to swing the mules around, but Travis's companion reined his horse into their path, blocking them.

"I had heard that you were with the Barbee drive," Travis said. "I didn't believe it at first. But it adds up. I understand you have quite a financial interest in that herd. Around thirteen hundred head."

"Yes," Lisa said, trying to show him a calmness.

Travis gestured. "I've got some six thousand head out there, give or take a few. I'm sure you noticed that."

"I did," Lisa said.

"I picked up a second herd a week ago on the Concho. Bought it, future payment, from a drover who was starting for Colorado, hoping to find a market. He preferred my price, six dollars a head, to taking a chance on selling in the north."

He added, "I'm taking them to Nevada."

Lisa realized she was in the deepest of trouble. In Travis was an ugly lawlessness. She seized up the whip, intending to lash the mules into motion and run down the rider ahead, but Travis grasped her wrist, forcing her back in the seat.

"Where are you going, Elizabeth?" he asked jeeringly.

"To find our camp," she said. "They'll be searching for me by this time. You know that. Get your hands off me."

"You'll be better entertained, staying with us for the night," Travis said. "I'll promise that you'll not find it dull."

Lisa spoke to the rider who was blocking the mules. "Get out of the way."

"For a woman who used her shape to outsmart me in a cattle deal, you're being a little aloof," Travis said.

Lisa wrested free from him suddenly and brought the whip down on the withers of his horse. The animal reared and went to pieces, nearly unseating Travis. That activity startled the mules, and also upset the mount of the other horseman.

Lisa used the whip on the mules. They burst away from the unshaven rider and broke into a frightened gallop. But the man mastered his horse quickly, swung alongside and seized her by the left arm. She clung to the seat with her other hand, trying to retain the reins, but that was too much for her and they fell loose.

She could not hold him off. He was beginning to drag her bodily from the wagon onto the horse with him. Her first thought was that she was in for humiliation. But there was a savagery in him, an indifference to injury of her, that terrified her. The horrifying thought came that this man did not care whether she remained alive.

She tried to reach the pistol but failed. The mules were running wild now, but her captor continued to spur his galloping horse close alongside while he drew her toward him.

Another rider came out of the dusk and overtook them. He shouted, "Let her go, Coe."

The arrival was Matthew Barbee. He was galloping at the man's stirrup. Lisa was released so suddenly she fell back, nearly plunging from the moving wagon. She grasped the seat and hung on.

The man had twisted in the saddle to face Matthew. They were in this position, the three of them abreast, the wagon bounding over the bunchgrass, Matthew knee to knee with the unshaven rider.

In the darkness Lisa saw the man trying to draw his pistol. But he was off balance and Matthew had drawn his own six-shooter ahead of him. Matthew brought the muzzle of his weapon down on the man's arm, knocking the pistol flying into the darkness as it came from the holster.

Matthew wrapped his arms around his opponent and both left the saddle, Matthew dragging his quarry with him. They struck the ground, rolling over twice. The man fought for a moment, but he had taken the worst of the fall and his right arm had been numbed by the blow Matthew had dealt.

Lisa managed to retrieve the dangling reins as the tired mules slowed. She pulled them to a stop in time to see the finish. It was a bloody one. Matthew had surged partly to his feet. He drove his fist into his opponent's face. He struck again a third time. In the darkness, Lisa could not see the effect of these blows but, sickly, she could visualize the damage.

Matthew released the man, letting him slump on his back. Matthew came to his feet. Kemp Travis now rode up, having quieted his horse. He held a six-shooter, but Matthew still had his pistol in his hand. Matthew stood in bitter and taut readiness to fire. He said, "I ought to do it, Kemp. Mauling a woman. That's a hanging offense."

Travis did not force the issue. He lowered his pistol. He said nothing, merely sitting there, as though he was aware that he was safe as long as he made no move.

"Are you hurt?" Matthew asked Lisa, without lifting his attention from Travis. "Can you handle the mules?"

"I'm all right," she said.

Matthew backed to his horse and mounted. He spoke to Travis. "Don't try to bring bad luck on us. We operate on the principle of an eye for an eye. Our bad luck will be yours, too."

He addressed Lisa. "Let's pull out."

Lisa swung the team abreast of him. They headed away, leaving the battered man lying there and Kemp Travis still sitting on his horse in the darkness.

Lisa's hands were cold. She sat limp, without strength. "I fell to daydreaming," she explained. "When I came down to earth, I was lost."

"Daydreaming gives wings to humans so that they can fly away from dust and heat and the sound and smell of cattle for a time," he said.

"How did you find me?" she asked.

"I picked up your trail before dark," he explained. "We missed you before sundown. Are you sure you're all right?"

"Yes. Did I hear you call that man by the name 'Coe'?"

"That was Coe Slade," Matthew said. "He's generally around when Kemp's trying to throw his weight."

"I had a terrible feeling that Coe Slade wanted to strangle me," Lisa said.

She told Matthew about the second herd Travis had acquired. "He evidently is still determined to take over all of the Diehl & Diehl contract," she said.

After that they rode in silence for a long time. Presently Matthew fired two shots, which was the signal that she had been found. Lisa heard a response far in the distance.

Their wagon fire appeared ahead. Men came riding to meet them. Hester appeared on foot, waiting.

Afterward Lisa sat on a wagon box by the fire, drinking coffee, and began to shake. Abel rode in and dismounted. He had been searching for her also.

He and Matthew and Paul walked aside and talked. He

returned presently and sat on his heels by the fire, accepting a plate of food from Hester.

He spoke to Lisa. "When anything like that happens, it's best to stop right where you are an' just set tight, rather than get spooky an' run in circles. We'll find you."

"I know that now," she said. "I was scared, however."

Lisa waited. When he did not speak, she said, "I expected more than that."

"More?"

"To be chastised," she explained. "I caused a lot of trouble."

He gave her a look. "Maybe you thought you'd have your eyelids sewed together so you'd learn to stay with the bunch?"

Before Lisa could answer, Shadrack, who had been with the remuda, came riding into the firelight. "Abel," he called. "I got a hawss down. It's thet gelded roan in Tom Zook's string. I'm afeared it's a broken laig. Lot o' dog holes out there, an' the roan was friskin' around. You better take a look."

Abel had taken only a bite or two of food. He laid the plate aside, walked to his horse and rode away with Shadrack.

After a time a pistol shot thudded in the darkness. The eating and the talk stopped, then resumed hastily.

Abel returned, and Hester handed him his plate again, which she had kept warmed. His mouth was taut, and Lisa noticed that his hand quivered just a little. He ate in silence. Lisa saw Hester pause beside him, saw the way her hand briefly, comfortingly caressed his head.

Always the responsibility was his, Lisa reflected, even to the bitter necessity of putting a crippled animal out of its misery.

Afterward, as Lisa was helping Hester with the chores, Abel spoke to her alone. "Matt mentioned that him—he—an' Coe Slade had a tussle. How bad was it?"

Lisa found herself reluctant to add to his burden, but it was necessary. "They fought hard. Very hard. Coe Slade tried to draw a pistol. Matthew beat him with his fists. It was bad enough."

He spent a lot of time fetching out and biting off the end of one of his thin stogies, a box of which he kept in the supply wagon, and of which he limited himself to one each evening. "I was afeared it was that way," he murmured, musingly. She understood that he was voicing his thoughts. He looked toward Matthew, who lay on his blankets, boots off, his saddle as a backrest and his night horse picketed where it would be quickly available. Matthew was reading a worn copy of Byron's works, squinting in the uncertain light of the fire. Coe Slade was farthest from his mind at the moment.

Abel drew absently on the cold stogie. Lisa brought a burning twig from the fire and held it to the tobacco. He tasted the smoke gratefully.

He suddenly realized it was she who had extended the courtesy. His mind returned from the dark channel it had been following. She saw that he was surprised.

"Muchas gracias!" he said.

"De nada," she replied. "It is nothing."

He eyed her, his quizzical smile appearing. She nodded. "I am learning too. Many things, in addition to a little Spanish from Ygnacio."

CHAPTER 15

Lisa halted the mules and stared, consternation growing within her. Before her lay a river that was a wild sweep of swirling water the color of the barren red banks that enclosed it.

The distance to the low-lying west shore seemed impossibly far. An upboil in the muddy current brought to the surface the swollen carcass of a drowned buffalo. This was driven against a cutbank downstream and there it wedged, held by the strength of the river. What driftwood there was, bobbed and waved jagged arms from the rolling surface. Some of it must have come from mountains far to the north, for its evergreen type was alien to this land.

This then was the Pecos River, and now she knew the reason for the tension that had been increasing daily among the crew. This was Horsehead Crossing, the only feasible ford for miles along this lonely stream.

This was why the soft-spoken Shadrack had handed her a letter that morning which he had asked that she keep until they reached a mailing point. "It's to my mother back in Tennessee," he had explained.

With a chill, she knew that letter was to be mailed only in case Shadrack was not alive.

Micah Jones had turned over to her a gold watch for safekeeping, along with a bottle of fine, aged whiskey.

"The loss of either would sadden me," he had told her. "Both are possessions to bolster the pride. The watch is to remind me that I had parents who were proud to reward a son on the day of his graduation from one of our better institutions of learning, the bottle to prove that I still have a vestige of forbearance. The watch I have been tempted to pawn many times, the whiskey to drink. I have refrained. If anything should detain me on the trail, both are yours, Elizabeth, the watch to admire, the liquor to quaff in my honor. And dear lady, if you do open this prized flask, forget for once your sheltered upbringing and get scandalously soused as a favor to me."

"I know what you mean," Lisa had said.

"She'll do no such thing," Hester had exploded. "My land, I never heard of such a disgraceful request!"

Lisa could understand all these things now and also why Abel, after riding ahead alone to the river the previous day, had returned and ordered the herd thrown off the trail in a dry camp, although it had been just past noon.

"I want 'em thirsty enough to be in a hurry to get to water tomorrow," he had explained. "We'll never let 'em change their minds. We'll hit the river on the run in the mornin' light with the sun at their backs, so thet they can see the far shore. More than one herd's been lost because the sun was in the eyes o' the cattle durin' a crossin'."

All these things were clear to her now, but it also seemed clear that their fears had been unnecessary. This crossing was impossible, of course. They would have to wait here until the Pecos fell. She had visualized a river ford as a peaceful scene with lowing cattle to their knees in grateful coolness, and horses splashing back and forth, bearing unhurried riders. This, no doubt would be the way it would be when they finally crossed. This evil thing that now barred their path would die when the freshet subsided, and they would wade its channel leisurely.

She looked at Hester, who sat nearby on the seat of the chuckwagon, gazing at the river. Something in Hester's demeanor brought a doubt. The dread returned. Hester's skin was as gray as a shroud. There was terror in her heart.

Lisa turned, shaken, and stared back. The herd was coming up, tightly bunched. Paul came galloping ahead and to the wagons. He had a bundle of boots on his arm and a collection of gunbelts and six-shooters over the saddlehorn. These he tossed into the hoodlum wagon.

"This is no place for a lady," he said. "We're all going to have to go over more than half naked."

"You're not going to risk trying to cross this—this awful river now?" Lisa exclaimed.

"It will be higher tomorrow and might stay up for weeks," he said. "Abel says we can't delay. I advise you to move to a more respectable distance."

He headed back to the herd, pulling off his shirt as he rode. Lisa swung the mules and drove away, along with Hester in the chuckwagon.

They pulled up at a distance and alighted, watching as the herd came up. The riders were yelling and swinging rope ends. Their shirts and breeches were tied around their shoulders and they rode only in their underwear.

The herd broke into a trot. It was a ponderous force as

elemental as the river itself. Alongside it the riders were tiny and seemed pathetically inadequate. They were frail and desolate humans, Lisa realized. They were afraid, and some of them knew the apprehension of death itself. But whatever the shrinking in their hearts, they rode steadily ahead in their nakedness. If they were to die, they were to go with the knowledge that their pride had not been damaged.

Paul led the way, followed by Shadrack with the remuda. Paul was mounted on a mouse-colored horse, a *grulla* she had heard Ygnacio describe it. It had a big stomach. She knew now why all the riders had been so selective in roping out particular horses from their strings for this task. These mounts, she now comprehended, were the ones they depended on for their skill in the water.

Hester stood silently watching, the grayness more pronounced in her skin. Paul sent his horse into the river. The remuda, flanked by Shadrack, followed without hesitation. Soon they were in swimming water and the current had its way with them, the bobbing heads stringing out and curving downstream.

The point of the herd, guided by Micah Jones and Ygnacio, came down to the ford at a steady trot and was given no chance to refuse. The cattle plunged in, floundered to their knees, then to their bellies. They began swimming. The sun reflected from their horns and Lisa could hear their snorting and bellowing.

The drive flowed steadily into the river. Lisa saw Matthew, on swing, enter the ford. The main body of the herd was in the water now. Paul was nearing the far shore. The current had carried him nearly a quarter of a mile downstream.

Lisa uttered a thankful sigh. Paul's horse had reached shallow water. Paul rode onto dry land. The remuda made it also, the horses lurching ashore, with Shadrack and Paul riding to control them.

The herd leaders reached safety also. Cattle began to splash ashore and scatter along the margin, blowing and lowing. The river was bridged by a wide ribbon of floating animals. Lon Melton and Nephi were in midstream and in swift current, on either flank of the herd, their horses swimming.

The drag entered the river, driven by Abel and Tom Zook. Hester spoke in a strangled voice and pointed. A wedge of cattle, caught by an eddy or some break in the current, was sweeping down upon Nephi. These steers were panicky and scrambling over each other for support. Nephi, occupied with trying to turn back other animals, was unaware of his danger.

Abel was standing in the stirrups, spurring his horse into swimming water. Lisa could not hear his voice at that distance above the overtone of bellowing from the cattle, but knew he was shouting a warning.

Milling cattle surrounded Nephi. Frantic animals, rearing, striking with their hooves, drove his horse under. Nephi also vanished.

He came to the surface for a moment in an opening among the thrashing steers. Lisa screamed wildly. Nephi, it was evident, could not swim!

She saw that Abel had left his horse and was stroking frantically toward the scene. He was the only one within reaching distance. Cattle blocked his route and he pulled himself over their wet backs. At one point the Longhorns were massed so compactly that he rose bodily out of the water and leaped from one to another before plunging into the river again.

Nephi grasped the horns of a steer. This kept him above water for a time, but the animal went under, carrying him with it. He returned once more to the surface, splashing and clawing frenziedly. He sank again.

Abel reached the spot a moment later and dove. Hester kept saying hysterically, over and over, "Abel! Oh, Abel!"

Around the spot where the two men had vanished cattle floundered and milled, and some were drowning.

Again Lisa drew a deep sigh. Two heads had appeared. Abel had Nephi in his arms and was fighting his way clear of the swirl of cattle. Nephi's horse emerged in the open also. Abel grasped its tail and the animal towed them toward the west shore.

Paul came galloping along the margin and rode into the river, swinging his lariat. His cast sailed within reach of Abel's arms, and he pulled them to safety.

The two of them lay on the shore for a time, Paul standing over them. Presently Abel arose. Then Nephi.

"Nephi ought to learn to swim," Hester said, trying to be matter-of-fact. "It was lucky Abel could get to him."

The scattered cattle milled in the river. The majority made it to the far shore. A hundred or more returned to the bank from which they had started. A few did not make either shore. Soon Horsehead Crossing was clear again, the river rolling silently past. Lisa saw more carcasses lodged against the cutbank downstream, along with that of the buffalo.

She tried to climb into the wagon. She found her strength

unequal to it. She had to lean against the wagon for a time before her nerves stopped quivering.

"Damn all cattle!" she said aloud.

Abel and Matthew and other riders returned, bringing a raft which they had improvised of driftwood. The cattle that had retreated to the east side were hazed into the river and forced to make it across. The wagons were lightened, and their contents were rafted to the far shore separately. The mules were led, swimming, astern of the raft.

It was deep twilight when Lisa stepped ashore on the west bank of the Pecos.

"How many did we lose, Abel?" Hester asked.

"Not much more'n a dozen is my guess," he said. "We'll tally out when it's convenient, to make sure."

In camp that night Nephi, his return from the shadow of death apparently already forgotten, was laughing and playing a tune in jigtime on his mouth harp. Ygnacio Valdez had Hester splint a broken forefinger which he had sustained, he knew not how or when, during the stress of the day. He displayed his bandaged injury as though it were a huge joke.

Matthew read again from his Byron, and dreamed his golden dreams. Shadrack came to Lisa and asked, shame-faced, for the letter he had written. It was as though to have penned that message to his mother was a weakness that must be concealed, now that the immediate fear of doom was forgotten. When she handed him the envelope he thrust it hastily in the pocket of his saddle jacket and hurried away.

Micah Jones, without shame or apology, reclaimed his watch and the cherished bottle of liquor. "We'll drink it when we hit Reno," he declared.

Paul shaved meticulously, preened himself and bided his time until he was able to trap Lisa alone when she was arranging cooking gear at the rear of the chuckwagon. He kissed her on the lips when she turned, suddenly aware of his nearness.

He tried to draw her closer, but when she merely stood passively looking at him, he released her. He laughed. "You've got to weaken sometime, Elizabeth," he said. "You're not ice, you're fire. I know that. You know it, too."

A deep and heavy sound arose in the night. Lisa, in the first instant, thought it was the beginning of a distant peal of thunder, although there was no cloud in the sky. The sound increased to a heavy rumble. In the next breath she knew that it was the herd! The cattle were running.

Paul raced toward his horse. Abel and all the men were in the saddle and gone, speeding through the darkness toward the stampede before she reached the open firelight.

She and Hester stood listening. The roar reached its peak and then faded rapidly into the distance. It became for a time a murmur that was the prey of the wind. Finally even this ended. Silence came.

Hester spoke, and it was as though she had not been breathing for all those minutes. "It was a bad run. What could have spooked the critters, tired as they was?"

They waited. They busied themselves tidying the camp. Hester got out her sewing basket and tried to put her mind to mending garments, but her hands kept shaking. Lisa also got her needle and thread and repaired a dress she had torn on cactus at a place called Johnson's Creek, a barren and lonely watercourse that was now far on their back-trail.

Two hours passed. Three. It was past midnight when they heard riders coming. The arrivals came into the firelight, and Lisa saw the way Hester's eyes sped from figure to figure.

Abel was there. And Matthew.

Abel looked at his mother and saw the question in her face. "Everybody's accounted for," he said. "Paul stayed with the herd, along with Nephi, Shadrack an' Tom. The bunch hung together pretty well until we got 'em stopped. What few skittered away ought to be easy to find come daybreak."

"What started 'em?"

Abel did not answer that. He walked to the wagon, got out his bedroll and threw it on the ground.

It was not until the next morning that Lisa heard an answer. It was while she and Hester were serving a late breakfast at mid-morning to tired and dusty riders who had succeeded in rounding up the scattered cattle.

She noticed a folded section of canvas lying beside the supply wagon. It had not been there a short time earlier. She picked it up, puzzled. The daily routine of packing and unpacking the gear had made her familiar with every item in both wagons. This was a wagon sheet, fairly new, but showing the first signs of weathering. It did not belong.

She turned and started to frame a question. Abel had been watching her, and spoke first. "Put it in the wagon. We'll keep it with us."

He dropped his empty plate and coffee tincup into the wreckpan. He spoke to Hester in the reluctant manner of a son who feels that he owes an explanation. "Thet wagon sheet was used to start 'em runnin' last night," he said.

"Somebody rode along the fringe of the herd, wavin' it, then let it go flyin' on the wind into the midst of them. The only other wagons thet we know about within reach of us are Kemp Travis's. Somebody from his outfit was waitin' for us on this side of the river."

He walked away to catch up his first day horse from the remuda Shadrack was bringing up.

Within half an hour camp was broken and the wagons were in motion. Well ahead of them, the herd was stringing out, still nervous as an aftermath of the stampede but beginning to settle down to the routine of the march.

The wagons reached higher ground and Lisa looked back. Beyond the river she could see a herd moving toward the crossing and nearby it a second drive closely held.

Abel rode to share her viewpoint and sat gazing. "The river must be even higher today," Lisa said. "They can't make it across, can they?"

"Travis will make it," Abel said. "He's got two crews to help with. He'll make it or die. He's goin' to stick with us like the curse of hell."

Later in the day and half a dozen miles farther on, from another rise in the land, she looked back and saw the ant-like movement of cattle and riders west of the river. Travis was succeeding in crossing his herds.

The day advanced. The slow miles passed, step by step, jolt by jolt, creak by creak. The sun beat down. A hot and arid wind came screaming at them at mid-afternoon, blowing dust and sand. The herd drifted with the wind eastward into rough, broken country along the river, in spite of all efforts by the riders. The wind died suddenly at sundown and the Longhorns settled down to grazing quietly. But they had lost five miles.

Lisa was finishing the chores in camp after the late meal that night, when she paused. Once again that low and deep rumble had arisen in the darkness.

This time the sound came from far away—so far she decided it might only be her imagination. She looked around. Matthew had been sitting on his blankets, his volume of odes open before him on his knees, but he had not been reading. A dead cigarette in his lips, he was listening to that muted murmur.

Nephi had been playing a soft and sad tune on his harp, but stopped now. There was melancholy resignation in the way he sat slumped, his eyes on the ground. Micah Jones was whittling aimlessly on a length of firewood. Lon Melton was swallowing hard and often, his Adam's apple bobbing in his thin neck. Al Quirk, contrary to his nature, had not said a word all evening, and was now very uneasy and nervous.

Lisa, accustomed to the routine, knew that Ygnacio and Tom Zook were on the cocktail trick with the herd, and that Shadrack was with the remuda. Only Abel and Paul were unaccounted for. She realized now that they had not even appeared for the meal.

She walked to the supply wagon, lifted the flap and peered in. The folded length of wagon sheet that had been used to stampede their own herd the previous night was missing.

She dropped the flap. Hester was gazing at her, tired but grim. Hester said nothing.

It was more than two hours before Abel and Paul returned. They picketed their night horses and walked into the circle without speaking. They silently ate the food Hester and Lisa handed them.

Later, after she and Hester were lying on their pallets in the supply wagon, Hester spoke in a whisper. "It had to be done. If we didn't hit back, Kemp Travis would have kept stampedin' us 'til we'd have lost every head of stock."

Lisa knew that no one in camp really slept that night. Abel doubled the guard on the herd, with the shifts alternating each three hours.

The night passed without trouble. In the morning, after they were on the trail again, Lisa saw evidence of scattered cattle being rounded up far behind them in the flats west of the river. Both of Kemp Travis's herds had been stampeded.

CHAPTER 16

Toward mid-afternoon, two riders appeared on a skyline to the south. They halted their horses and remained there, plainly visible, for a time, watching as the drive crawled ahead.

They were too far away to identify with the unaided eye. Hester brought out a small brass telescope. "Kemp Travis an' Coe Slade," she told Lisa.

After a time the pair wheeled their horses and rode away. They had made no hostile move or gesture, but the threat was plain enough. They were promising retaliation.

Their appearance had its effect. Al Quirk left his place on swing and rode to the wagon Lisa was driving, saying he was out of tobacco and wanted to replenish his pouch from the supply he had in his war sack. She halted the wagon for a moment to accommodate him but remained on the seat, not interested in his activities.

But as Quirk mounted to return to the herd, Abel came riding up and intercepted him. "Where's your gun?" Abel asked.

Lisa was a little frightened by something in Abel's voice. She saw that Quirk had once again removed the six-shooter with which Abel had supplied him, and no doubt had hidden it in the wagon.

"I didn't hire out to git mixed up in any shootin' scrapes," Quirk said.

"A gun is for your own safety," Abel said. "As long as you've got one on, you can defend yourself. In addition, you hired out to help get these cattle to Nevada."

"They ain't my cattle," Quirk said. "I'm askin' to be paid off. I'm goin' back to San Ysidro. I seen Kemp Travis out there. Slade was with him. This drive ain't never goin' to make it to Reno. You know that as well as I do, Abel."

Abel rode to the chuckwagon. Hester delved into a leather satchel and brought out a canvas bag which contained their meager cash supply. From this, Abel counted out two gold-pieces and some silver which he gave to Quirk.

"Turn your horse in with the bunch," he said.

Quirk was suddenly ashen. "But I'll need a horse. I'll pay for it."

"We've got none to spare," Abel said. "We're likely to be on short string before we git to Nevada. I don't have to tell you thet."

Quirk was breathing hard. "I've changed my mind. I'll string along."

"We don't want a man thet changes point with every swing o' the wind," Abel said. "Get off the horse."

"You wouldn't put a man afoot out here, Abel? Not way out here? It's a hundred miles to nowhere."

"You can make it to the stage road in a day or so walkin'," Abel said. "You'll be picked up."

"Comanches might git me. Or 'Paches!"

Abel rode alongside Quirk. "Get down!" he commanded.

Quirk slowly, fearfully slid to the ground. Abel stripped the saddle and headstall from the man's mount and tossed them at his feet. He mounted his own animal and sent the loose horse away with a slap, heading it toward the remuda.

He looked at his mother and Lisa. "Git rollin'."

Up to that moment Lisa had believed he would relent. "You can't leave him like this!" she protested. "Alone! On foot!"

Abel rode alongside the wagon and used the end of his lariat to startle the mules into motion.

Lisa leaned back on the reins, hauling them to a quick stop. "Give him a horse and enough food and water to carry him through, at least."

"No," he said. He brought the rope slashing down again on the mules. Hester released the brake and the chuckwagon began moving. Abel galloped away to rejoin the herd.

Lisa looked back. Al Quirk was a forlorn and frightened mote amid the immensity of the barren plain.

She prevailed on Hester to halt. From the foodboxes she made up a pack, along with a filled canteen, which Quirk came hurrying to accept.

Abel saw this and came galloping back. There was an unyielding set to his features. She sensed that he was on the point of smashing the canteen and scattering the food. She stood between his wrath and Quirk. For seconds they faced each other in a clash of wills.

Suddenly he turned and rode away. She had overruled his judgment and he had been forced to accept it.

As she drove the wagon away, Al Quirk burst into a frenzy of fury. He cursed Abel. He even cursed Lisa. When she looked back, he was still standing there, screaming imprecations and shaking his fist.

"It's cruel!" Lisa choked. "Cruel! Brutal!"

Tears streaked Hester's cheeks, but there was a fierce light in her eyes and almost a scorn in her voice. "Do you think Abel wanted to do that? But he had to. This ain't Chicago. You can't call on the law to help you out here. Abel did what had to be done. We've got to stand up to Kemp Travis. If any of us show we're scared, none of us will get out of this alive. Not one person, not one head o' stock. Kemp's gone too fur, an' he's got too much money at stake to back down. Don't you understand that even yet, Elizabeth? Kemp's out to smash us. If he can sell that second herd of his along with the other one, it means he'll be a rich man. A rider's got no more right to quit a herd out here than a soldier has to desert his post, or a sailor to abandon his ship."

Nephi did not play his harp in camp that night. Matthew lay with his book before him, but Lisa knew that he found no joy in the printed words.

No one spoke to Abel. He was apart from them, remote even from his brother. Matthew believed his action had been too harsh. Once again, Lisa saw the way Hester's hand touched Abel's hair, tenderly, soothingly.

From the darkness, at long range, a rifle opened up. Paul Drexel, who was nearest Lisa, pushed her down into the uncertain protection of the wagon wheels.

She heard bullets ripping through the canvas tilts of both wagons. The sounds were harsh and slapping. A second rifle joined in. Splinters flew as struts were nicked.

The firing stopped. After a time the faint echo of riders departing at a steady gallop came in from the night.

Abel got to his feet and stood listening. Presently he turned and looked at Matthew.

No word was spoken. Matthew laid aside his book and pulled on his boots. Paul Drexel, his smile tight and fixed on his lips, also got to his feet. The two of them walked to their night horses and methodically heaved the cinches tight and laced the latigos.

Abel got two rifles from the supply wagon and handed them to the two men. Hester lifted a protesting hand, opened her lips to voice a plea.

Abel spoke. "Shoot high, like they did. They're not on the kill—yet. Neither are we. But notch low enough to show 'em thet we'll notch lower if need be."

Hester's hand dropped helplessly, her protest unspoken. Matthew, without looking at her, rode away with Paul to carry on the contest that was building up between Abel and Kemp Travis, a contest that, up to now, was one of nerves, of feint and counter-feint to test out the full temper of the other's will.

This time Abel was sending his brother into danger.

Abel beckoned Micah and they moved apart. Abel had in his hand the lesson books. Their voices droned on as they went over some grammatical point that he was bent on conquering.

And, Lisa told herself, conquer it he would. He was mastering education with the same determination with which he was driving this herd of cattle westward.

According to the swing of the Big Dipper in the sky, it was past midnight when Matthew and Paul returned. Lisa was still awake. She knew that Hester also had not closed her eyes.

Abel, too, had not turned in. He was sitting close by the faint fire-glow, the textbook in his hand.

Lisa heard him speak. "Any trouble?"

Matthew answered casually. "They threw some lead in our direction, but none of it counted. I put a couple of loads into their fire. That slowed 'em down."

Paul spoke. "It'll get worse before it gets better."

After that there was silence. Lisa finally slept. But when Nephi came in from the graveyard shift and scratched on the wagon sheet to awaken them to their cooking duties, she knew that Hester had lain there all night, staring up into the empty darkness.

The loss of Al Quirk left a serious vacancy, short-handed as they were. Abel announced his decision at breakfast. He looked at Hester. "Hate to ask it of any woman, 'specially of one with two growed sons, but if you could hold down second swing, it'd help."

Hester nodded. "I've been thinkin' the same thing. The herd is handlin' easy. I can turn back drifters as good as a man. Done it before. Get out my sidesaddle, Abel. It's in a gunnysack in the wagon."

Lisa found Abel's gaze upon her. "Thet means hookin' the wagons up, tandem," he said. "We'll lighten load as much as possible so that three spans can handle 'em. If need be, we'll abandon the hoodlum wagon. Can you handle it?"

"I could," Lisa said. "But I'm the one to ride with the cattle." She walked to Hester and kissed the elder woman on the cheek. "Hester has the savvy," she said. "But I have the advantage in weight, and in age. Hester's had her day at riding saddleback with cattle. She is the one to stay with the wagons."

Once again she saw the flicker of approval in his eyes. "It

was what I was thinkin'. You're promoted from cook's swamper to full trail hand. Thirty a month an' keep."

Within a few minutes Lisa, now a trifle frightened, was with the cattle. She was mounted on a small gray horse, fitted with a worn sidesaddle that belonged to Hester.

The position Abel assigned her was the second swing on the right flank of the column. Ahead of her in the first swing was Lon Melton, and beyond Melton, Paul rode at point. Her partner on the opposite flank was Nephi. He grinned encouragingly at her across the backs of the cattle.

"These here ol' whangeroos has been as tame as sheep as a rule," he shouted. "But you never know what they'll do next. If they take it in their heads to skitter you jest stand aside, Missy 'Lisabeth. Jest stand aside. Let us men do the ridin'."

The cattle did not skitter that day. Nor the next. Nor the next. Each day became a replica of its predecessor, and a forecast of its successor. Out of the warm blankets in the brittle chill of first daylight and to the herd with the crew where, at Abel's command, she remained at a safe distance while he and the other riders hazed the cattle into motion. They called this the stretchout.

She learned that this was always a tricky moment. The cattle still had the memory of their home range in their minds. Particularly at this hour were they determined to head back in that direction rather than the way they were traveling.

This herd was trail-broke, but that was only a figure of speech. The Longhorns, still wild and unpredictable, marched westward only because a greater will was forced upon them. Abel was that will. The other men and herself were only the instruments of his planning.

Always at the stretchout there was the danger of stampede. And always Abel, riding hard, directing swing and point men with arm signals, anticipated and forestalled trouble. Always the cattle were outmaneuvered by him and molded into obedience. Always they plodded westerly against their own instinct.

Abel drove himself far harder than he drove the cattle or the other members of the crew. Mainly he was with the drag, pushing it along, but when danger cropped up elsewhere he was always on hand.

And so the days went by; stretchout at dawn, the slow and steady miles through the warming morning, the weary and hot distances of the afternoon. The same country, the same dry willows along the stream courses, the same greasewood, sage and juniper, the same flat-topped bluffs in the distance which they never seemed to reach, but which kept receding ahead of them into the depths of the mighty land.

Through all this they moved with treadmill monotony as guardians of the cattle. The ever-present cattle which filled their world. Lisa began to loathe them with a hot and helpless fury. And she resented the way Abel had dedicated all of them to seeing to the health and welfare of the beasts.

But at night she found herself springing awake at any unusual sound, and sitting taut and rigid in her blankets until sure the herd was safe. She began to despise even herself for this. She was being chained, link by link, to these bovine creatures. All she and the others lived for were the Longhorns. Like Abel, they were all slaves to the mass of dumb brutes that they guarded.

They had advanced deep into the territory of New Mexico and their course was now always directly west. Each night when they camped Abel placed markers that pointed to the North Star. On arising, this was the compass by which he set their course for the day, rain or shine.

Not since the nights of the retaliatory stampedes and exchange of warning bullets had they seen or been troubled by Kemp Travis or his men. They knew that Travis and his two herds were somewhere ahead of them now and a score of miles to the north of their route, for Travis had been driving hard since those clashes. Their last reports had him and his cattle some two days in advance of them.

Abel was content to maintain their own fifteen-mile average advance each day. "We aren't halfway," he said, "and with the hardest miles ahead. I aim to get to Nevada with some meat on the steers."

As the days passed, Lisa began to feel sure that the danger of further physical clash with Travis and his outfit was ended. She stated this belief to Abel.

"Maybe," was all he said. She realized that he did not share her hopes. The dread that had faded out of her mind edged back again.

If there was any such shadow on the thoughts of the riders it was submerged in a new anticipation. They were nearing the next river of importance, the Rio Grande, and beyond the crossing lay a town named Los Molinos, the first settlement they had encountered in weeks.

"They'll all likely get drunk as pigs in this Los Molinos," Hester had commented pessimistically to Lisa. "Men have got no sense at all."

CHAPTER 17

The prospect of escaping from the cattle and their bellowing and their smell, for even a few hours, was a tonic. Nephi's mouth harp came out of hiding and Shadrack danced a jig.

Even Abel relaxed and laid aside his textbooks and sat gazing into the campfire in the evenings. It came to Lisa that he was dreaming his dreams also.

The great day approached. They had half a dozen miles of easy trail to reach the river. There had been no rain in weeks, full summer had arrived, and the New Mexican landscape, with its mesas and buttes, its stunted brush and dry arroyos, lay hot and arid beneath a blazing sun.

Abel rode ahead to scout the Rio Grande. No trouble was anticipated and the general opinion was, as Tom Zook put it, "She won't be more'n fetlock deep on a green grasshopper."

Abel was gone two hours. He was long-faced and solemn as he came back and rode down the line. The word went around, shouted from rider to rider.

"Condemn it! The river's up. Swimmin' water, Abel says, an' plenty of it. Must have been a storm up in the mountains to the north."

Their high spirits died. Paul groaned and gazed ruefully at his garb. He had arrayed himself in his gaudiest saddle attire in anticipation of visiting the fleshpots of Los Molinos. So had all the other members of the crew. Now they were recalling that day at the Pecos River.

Lisa joined Hester at the wagons. There was a twinkle in Hester's eyes as she urged the mules ahead. "Come on, Elizabeth. There's goin' to be a lot of red-necked cowboys in these parts mighty soon."

They drew ahead of the herd. The course of the river came in sight. Lisa was certain she was seeing the sun reflecting on a wide expanse of water. This illusion persisted until they emerged into close view of the ford.

Lisa gazed blankly. The Rio Grande was far from in flood. What water there was flowed in shallow, sandy channels in the wide riverbed. The sun-blink she had seen came mainly from the hot faces of dry sandbars and flats.

Hester was laughing. "They'll skin Abel alive for this."

Lisa understood now, and began to giggle also. She led the way, saddleback, and Hester followed with the wagons. The water was little more than knee-deep on the horses at any point, and the bottom was solid.

As they neared the opposite shore they discovered that a score or more of Indian women were washing clothes and pounding them on rocks along the margin of the stream just below the ford.

"Zuni squaws," Hester said. "Or maybe Hopis. Abel said we'd likely run into them through this stretch. They're peaceful enough, provided you keep your eyes open."

The Indian women were at the river chiefly to gossip and pass the day. Appearance of the wagons and two women was an unexpected diversion. They came swarming to surround the arrivals, chattering and pointing and making remarks that evidently were not complimentary.

They fingered Lisa's dress and lifted her skirt, exclaiming at the whiteness of her skin above her stockings. She had to use the quirt to drive them away. Others were trying to climb into the wagon. Hester, infuriated, was fending them off. Lisa rode to her assistance.

They finally escaped from their predicament only by putting the mules to a gallop and placing distance between them.

"Well, they seemed harmless enough, even if they was bold as brass," Hester said as they recovered a measure of their dignity. "Praise the Lord they wasn't 'Paches. Otherwise they'd have tore us to pieces. They say 'Pache squaws are worse even than the braves."

The drive was coming up now. Lisa and Hester watched from a distance. Paul, his fine garb tied around his neck, wearing very little, led the herd to the margin of the water course and pulled up, staring disbelievingly. Micah Jones, on the opposite point, was also stripped to his underdrawers. The others on swing were in the same embarrassing situation.

Only Abel, far back with the drag, was fully clad. The hoodwinked men of the crew were gazing back at him, waving their arms and evidently shouting angry promises of retaliation.

"Lucky we can't hear what they're callin' him," Hester gasped, weak from laughter.

The Longhorns, impatient for water, were moving ahead with the unchangeable mass force of an avalanche. The nearly-naked riders had no alternative other than to stay with them.

The squaws again came hurrying to take in this new spectacle. They began laughing shrilly and pointing. Cowering men attempted futilely to cover themselves. They tried to drive their tormenters away with quirts and threats.

That had inflammatory effect. The squaws shouted taunts and insults in return. Paul Drexel, who was the first to face this new humiliation at close hand, sought to garb himself in his fine clothes as he rode.

The Indian women swarmed around him. A plump squaw dipped her hands in the mud of the river margin and splattered him with wet, red clay.

Other riders suffered the same fate. Dressing became impossible. The men finally abandoned peaceful means of subduing the screeching, jeering Indians. They leaped from the saddle and began hurling mud in retaliation.

That brought on a mud fight that lasted until both sides were plastered and exhausted. Lisa laughed until her throat ached. She discovered that Abel had crossed the river, staying clear of the contest, and had joined her. He was sitting hipshot in the saddle, a cigarette in his fingers, his eyes alight with high humor.

Hester finally stirred the mules and withdrew. Lisa and Abel rode side by side, following the wagons.

"The cattle?" she questioned.

"They'll stay on water," he said. "The boys will shove 'em out after they get rid o' the squaws. I wouldn't dare show my face around 'em before they cool down."

He added, "I'll pick out a bedground. We'll lay over here another day. It'll do us good, as well as the cattle. We've been hittin' it pretty steady since we left the Pecos."

They came in sight of Los Molinos. A score of buildings stood at the crossroads of stage and freighting trails. Beyond it, the walls of an Indian pueblo were pale yellow in the sun.

It was still mid-afternoon when the herd was turned out on grazing within sight of Los Molinos. The false fronts and flat roofs of the settlement might have been gilded spires and castle turrets, if the eagerness of the men was a yardstick.

The fiasco of the river crossing had put the riders in high spirits. They filled Abel's boots with water and hid a lizard in his hat while he was bathing in the stream. The horseplay went on. They had pushed the hardships of the back-trail out of their minds and were ignoring what lay ahead, for the time being at least.

This, Lisa realized, was what Abel had intended when he had brought about the absurdity at the river. She too found herself looking forward to enjoying whatever Los Molinos had to offer in the way of civilization.

"Four of you men will go in an' be back by ten o'clock tonight," Abel said. "The rest of us will have our turn then."

They drew straws for it. Matthew, Ygnacio Valdez, Micah Jones and Tom Zook were the lucky ones. Matthew, knowing the disappointment it was to Paul Drexel, offered to trade places.

Paul, smiling, refused. "Maybe the cards will be running better later on."

"Or maybe the gals will be more amenable," Micah Jones said. "I hear music. Where there's music, there's a female in spangles an' warpaint."

The four had bathed the mud from them and preened their town attire. They caught up the flashiest horses from their strings and mounted.

Lisa had also been busy in the hoodlum wagon, arraying herself. She came hurrying. "Wait, Matthew! I am going with you."

Matthew pulled up. "Not you?"

Hester tugged at Lisa's sleeve. "You ain't wanted, Elizabeth," she whispered. "Let 'em kick up their heels a little."

Lisa laughed. She climbed into the sidesaddle. "I won't follow you around, Matthew, or try to lead you away from the paths of temptation. I promise to strictly mind my own affairs and return to camp before sunset."

"Apparently there's no refusing you," Matthew sighed.

"All I ask is that I appear respectably escorted when I enter this place," she said. "My main object is to buy thread and needles and a thimble, all of which I lost somewhere between here and the Pecos. I also need a few items of clothing, the nature of which I will not divulge."

"I've seen 'em hanging on clotheslines," Matthew said.

"That'll do, both of you!" Hester exclaimed, red-faced. "Such talk. My land! What are young people comin' to?"

Lisa and the four men rode gaily into Los Molinos. The settlement dwindled at close range. There were no gilded towers. Shabby frame and 'dobe buildings straggled alongside the trail for a hundred yards or more.

There was one barroom, and from this came the tinny music of a hurdy-gurdy. The other three men pulled up there, but Lisa and Matthew galloped the length of the settlement. "Dragging the town," Matthew called it.

He half-drew his six-shooter. "Maybe we ought to shoot out a few windows," he threatened.

Lisa pleased him by squealing in mock alarm and struggling with him to force him to return the weapon to its holster. This brought them into close personal contact. Matthew suddenly pulled her closer. She saw that he intended to kiss her. She sobered, sudden memories returning and darkening this moment.

He understood. He drew back a little, but his hands still held her arms. He shook his head gravely. "Neither of us Barbees killed Frank O'Hara," he said. "Least of all Abel. Surely, Elizabeth, you must know us well enough by this time to know that?"

"Why Abel least of all?" she demanded.

He released her. "It's just something of which I'm sure," he said. "And I feel that some day you'll be sure, too."

He wheeled his horse. "I missed my chance to kiss a pretty girl. When will I get another?"

Lisa laughed and they were lighthearted again as they rode back to the core of the settlement. He helped her alight at the shoddy general store, which was named the Boston Emporium.

"Please don't get too boisterous in there," he admonished. "We're depending on you to uphold the dignity of the B-T crew."

"I'll carry my ginger pop like a lady," she promised.

She saw that all the levity was abruptly gone from Matthew. He was looking at something back of her. She turned.

Three men had stepped from the wagon tunnel of a livery barn some distance away and on the opposite side of the street. They were just in from the trail, for their rough saddle garb was worn and weather-faded and gray from the dust of miles. Their jaws bore a heavy bristle of beard and their hair was long and curling over the collars of their saddle coats.

One was Kemp Travis. He wore a holstered pistol. His companions carried braces of weapons. Lisa intuitively sensed that they had been waiting in the livery establishment for some time.

Travis and one of the men remained where they were, but the third member came across the street and stood on the clay sidewalk some fifty feet away, gazing at Matthew and Lisa.

His attitude aroused a clutching dread in Lisa. He was powerfully built, with high, box-like shoulders. His heavy growth of beard masked his features, and his wide-brimmed hat, weathered and drooping, shaded his eyes. Still there was something faintly familiar about him.

She looked at Matthew. A darkening shadow had formed in him. Some of the color had gone from his face.

Suddenly she knew! This rough, armed man was the one who had tried to humiliate her the evening she had been lost on the plains beyond the Pecos. This was Coe Slade who had taken a fist-beating at Matthew's hands.

Matthew spoke without looking at her. "I'll meet you later, Elizabeth."

Coe Slade was gazing at Matthew. She had never seen such deadly purpose in eyes. He had come here to kill Matthew in payment for the punishment he had taken that evening.

Slade spoke, lifting his voice so that his intention would be plain. "Well, if it ain't Matt Barbee an' the Chicago woman who couldn't wait to be a widow to get her hands on Frank O'Hara's ranch."

Matthew said, "Better start your buying, Elizabeth. You can do no good here."

He moved away from her and toward Slade. She overtook him and tried to link arms with him and walk with him.

"No!" she said desperately. "No, Matthew! You can't fight him! That's what he wants!"

Slade spoke again. "Don't try to hide back of skirts, Barbee."

Matthew looked at her, and she saw in him the impassable wall of a man's pride. He disengaged her fingers and pushed her toward a doorway. "Go in there," he commanded. "Get off the street!"

She seized him again, clinging, trying to place herself as a shield between him and Coe Slade.

A man wearing a clerk's apron ran from the Boston Emporium and carried her bodily back into shelter. "Lady, do you want to get killed . . . ?"

"No! Let me go!" But she could not break free from him.

Matthew was speaking. "All right, Slade! You're a liar and you know it. Take off your hat and tell Miss Randolph that you are."

Then they were shooting. It came and struck and passed with the violence of a thunderclap. Lisa saw Matthew die. She saw his body lift and give to the smash of Coe Slade's first bullet.

Slade had been sure of his superiority with a gun. Matthew had never before drawn a pistol in anger on a man. He was still trying to bring his weapon from the holster when Slade's bullet struck. He staggered, managed to lift his six-shooter and fire. His shot shattered a window somewhere beyond Slade.

A second bullet from Slade's gun struck him. And a third. These drove him reeling back, and he fell. He tried to pull himself to his knees and lift his pistol again. Slade shot him a fourth time.

Lisa tore free from the clerk's grasp and ran to Matthew's side. She huddled over him and screamed at Slade, "Stop it! Oh, stop it!"

Slade gazed at her for an instant over the pistol, and its bore was bearing upon her. It came to her that he was on the verge of shooting her down also, for there was a deadly implacability in him.

Kemp Travis shouted frantically, "For God's sake, Coe . . . !"

Slade lowered his pistol. He walked rapidly across the street and into the livery barn. Travis and the third man followed him.

Matthew was still alive. He looked up at Lisa and tried to say something. He couldn't make it. She guessed what he wanted.

She bent close and kissed him on the lips. "Matthew! Oh, Matthew!"

He smiled at her and managed to speak. "Kiss a pretty girl," he murmured.

He drifted away.

When Lisa finally looked up, she was surrounded by the staring faces of residents of Los Molinos. Avid curiosity was there, and some were laughing excitedly. This death meant little to them. Matthew was a stranger and they did not know the cause of his passing, nor did they care.

She came to her feet. Travis and his two men were riding out of town, galloping fast. "Stop them!" she demanded. "Stop that man! Coe Slade! It was murder!"

Nobody spoke or made a move to obey. They only looked at her woodenly. Micah Jones came bursting through the group. He dropped on his knees beside Matthew and said in an agonized voice, "Matt! Matt! Damn it to hell! Why did you tackle him? You knew you didn't have a chance!"

He looked up at Lisa. "Who's going to tell Hester?" he asked numbly.

Afterward Lisa sat in a room at the rear of the Boston Emporium. Micah and Ygnacio were with her. Abel, accompanied by Paul Drexel, had arrived in town on spent horses, a short time earlier, summoned by Tom Zook. She had seen them walk into the furniture and supply store, which also served as the undertaking establishment for the town. Matthew's body had been taken there.

Presently Abel came out alone and walked to the Boston Emporium. He came to the rear room and Micah admitted him. He seemed taller and thinner than ever, and his eyes were flat and without life.

"How'd it happen?" he asked Lisa.

She told him. She spoke slowly, carefully, searching her mind for details. "It was murder," she concluded. "They'll arrest Slade, of course."

He said, "They tell me that eyewitnesses call it self-defense. They say both Matt an' Slade went for their guns at the same time. They say it looked like they were settlin' an old grudge, an' both men were ready fer a fight."

"Slade forced it on Matthew," Lisa said exhaustedly. "Matthew had no other course."

"There's no law here, anyway," Abel said. "At least none that's interested in takin' up the feuds of Texas trail men. Slade is back with Travis's herds. They're camped a day's drive west. It looks like they been waitin' 'til we showed up. Slade rode back to Los Molinos today for one purpose—to get Matthew. There's more'n twenty men with Travis's wagons, they say. No peace officer would risk his hide tryin' to take Slade away from 'em, even if he was a mind to go out that far."

Micah spoke suddenly. "Don't you try it, either, Abel."

Abel looked at him. "We've still got the cattle on our hands. Other things can wait."

He turned to leave. "I've got to tell Hester. We kept it from her when Tom Zook rode out to fetch us."

It was after dark when she and Abel rode up to the wagons. Hester sat on a wagon box, her hands in her lap. She came to her feet as they dismounted and looked at Abel for a long time.

"It's Matthew, ain't it?" she finally asked. "I guessed it when I seen you ridin' away fast with Paul."

Abel nodded, and could not bring himself to speak. Hester came to him and struck him on the chest with her clenched fist. She began sobbing. "Why didn't you watch out for him, Abel? He was my youngest!"

She kept beating at Abel's chest with her fist, pounding out her helpless grief. He stood motionless, his hands on her shoulders.

Lisa moved in and took Hester in her arms. "It wasn't Abel's fault," she said, almost fiercely. "If anyone was to blame, I'm that person. It was because of me that Matthew was killed."

CHAPTER 18

Matthew was buried the next morning in a dreary grave-yard on the fringe of Los Molinos. Micah Jones, tired and thin of voice, read verses from the Book of John and led in the prayer. A hymn was sung. Lisa joined in, as did Paul, who stood at her side.

Hester did not lift her head. Abel stood with his arm around his mother, gazing straight ahead. There was a frozen sorrow in him that was beyond the reach of comforting words. And something dark and grim.

When the last prayer was said, Abel spoke to the open grave. "We'll come back, Matt, an' get you. We'll take you with us to wherever we settle."

The herd did not lay over the second night near Los Molinos, as Abel had intended. Within an hour after Matthew's funeral, the men threw the cattle on the trail and pointed them west again.

Soon the Longhorns were striding along at their customary pace, the dust was rising and the sun was burning down upon them. Los Molinos merged with the roll of the land behind them.

Hester kept looking back as long as the white cross over the fresh mound of earth was visible among the boulders and juniper on the hillside. Lisa watched Abel. Not until the last moment did he turn in the saddle and gaze in that direction. Then he rode ahead again with the cattle.

The drive marched westward. They traveled through a land where juniper grew thinly on the rocky slants. Mesas arose on either hand, their tops capped with an armor of lava which had eroded into talus slopes of tumbled rock that could hide a legion of foes.

Lisa had the sensation of invading a ghostly city. She rode with a loaded pistol strapped in a holster to her waist, and often with a rifle across the pommel, as did the others on Abel's orders.

She was now mounted astride, using Matthew's saddle. She

119

had remade her riding habit to suit the purpose. Abel, shocked, had raged and forbidden this breach of convention, but she had ignored him, and his protest had sputtered out.

She held the first swing position. She knew that she had been moved to this spot by Abel so that she would be under better observation by the majority of the crew. Even the point riders ahead of her had instructions to keep an eye on her and on Hester. Abel made sure that Hester kept the wagon very close to the herd.

But the days went by and no sign of life showed. The mesa country fell behind and the mountains began to peer at them from the north, some bearing a dapple of snow. They crossed the continental divide by way of a great sagebrush plain. The weather was cool and Abel let the Longhorns set their own pace. They followed a stream called the Rio Puerco. One day, at sundown, they bedded on a river which Abel said was the Little Colorado. It was a flat, meandering watercourse.

The carcasses of two Longhorns, ravaged by coyotes and magpies, lay on a flat near the stream. "Travis had his herds here about a week ago, from the sign," Abel told Lisa. "He's still pushin' his cattle. Beginnin' to lose a few."

The Little Colorado meant that they were entering the country of the Navajo, reputedly more peaceful than the Apaches. Lisa and the men relaxed a little. But Abel lectured them on the necessity of never giving up vigilance.

They had what seemed to be a bit of luck a few days after reaching the Little Colorado. Abel hired a rider from among a party of prospectors whom they encountered. The man, buck-toothed and shaggy, went by the name of Jim Starr.

Abel took it for granted that Lisa would be glad to return to the jolting wagon seat. He found that he was mistaken.

"Let Jim Starr drive the blasted mules," she told him. "I'm staying with the herd. That man doesn't act like he savvies cattle, anyway. He looks like he just got out of a cage."

"Out of prison, most likely," Abel acknowledged. He eyed her wonderingly. "Danged if I ain't beginnin' to think thet you like workin' cattle. Didn't I hear you use a few cuss words this mornin' when thet bunch-quittin' steer with the blaze on his forehead tried to break past you for about the tenth time?"

"I had reason," Lisa said. "He is a very aggravating beast."

He smiled in a superior manner. "Don't you remember thet one? He's the one whose eyelids I sewed one day so thet— that—he'd learn to stay with the herd. But a skinny no'thern female come along an' tried to interfere. Even wanted to use a horsewhip on me. I was weak enough to take out the thread after she pulled out. An' so the steer still causes work for cowhands, an' makes even a lady say words fer which she ought to git her mouth washed out with soap."

Lisa eyed him scornfully. "So I'm skinny?"

He inspected her from head to foot. "Come to think of it, you have rounded out here an' there since this drive started. Cow-camp grub seems to agree with you. An' you've turned as brown as a Kickapoo squaw."

"Are you tryin to say I'm fat and need a bath?" Lisa inquired. "I'll have you know I scrubbed myself in this confounded river only last night. As for being fat——"

"What do you mean, you took a bath in the river. Alone?"

"Well, I should rather think so," she said indignantly.

He was angry now. "Kain't—can't—I git it through your head thet it's dangerous to wander out of camp by yourself?"

"If you think——!" She saw how hopeless it was to continue along that line. She returned to the subject that had brought on this clash. "I'm going to stay with the herd."

She again had her way. But when Jim Starr learned that he was to be relegated to driving mules while a female intruded upon a masculine prerogative, he quit forthwith and hurried away to overtake the prospecting party.

Abel blamed her. "Stubborn female!" he said scathingly.

"Good riddance!" she sniffed. "I'd rather have had a bear around the cattle."

It was sundown, two days after the dispute over Jim Starr, when Abel gave the signal to throw off. Shadows were long and turning purple on the flanks of the mountains to the north.

The wheeling motion that swerved the herd from the route of march onto the bedground for the night was the only maneuver the cattle obeyed willingly and with little need of attention from the riders.

Lisa left the herd, as customary, when this routine activity began, and galloped toward the wagons to help Hester with the evening meal.

Hester had disobeyed Abel's instructions, for once, and had driven the wagons nearly a mile ahead to a grove of willows along the stream.

The terrain seemed to be a flat, unbroken expanse of thin sagebrush, but Lisa found that this was deceptive and that she had descended into a swale and was momentarily out of view of both the herd and the wagon. Furthermore a barranca, with six-foot cutbanks, cut across her path. The barranca was dry now. She found a crossing point and leaped her horse to the sandy bottom.

As she did so, dark-faced, savage figures surrounded her. They were Apaches! She tried to scream, but hands dragged her from the horse and a blow on the side of the head from a palm half-stunned her.

She attempted to cry out again. A hand was thrust over her mouth, and she sank her teeth into it. Another blow dazed her.

She revived. She was being half-carried—dragged, rather —and mainly by the hair. Pain impelled her to regain her feet. They were squatty, broad-faced men with animal-like coarse hair. Some had bandeaus around their heads and the majority wore loose cotton blouses, buckskin breeches and a type of stiff legging around their thighs. One had on an army jacket, with only a breechclout below.

Their gaze was flat, utterly impersonal. This, above all, shriveled her hope, brought home the knowledge that to them her life was a matter of complete indifference.

She tore free from the one who grasped her—more by the surprise of sudden action than her own strength. She ran, but she was overtaken before she had taken half a dozen steps.

A hand seized the back of her blouse, for she had left her saddle jacket bundled on the horse during the heat of the day. The blouse ripped away, along with her chemise.

Naked to the waist, she was hurled to the ground. Grimy hands savagely muffled her attempt to scream, and she was again kicked and beaten until she could only gasp.

They dragged her to her feet and she was prodded and kicked into staggering along with them at a half-run. She looked back. She could see the glow of sundown on the mountains. They had emerged from the barranca and were traveling southwest away from those mountains. She could not see the herd or the wagons.

Darkness was coming fast. She gave herself up for lost.

In the dusk Abel, accompanied by Micah Jones, Shadrack and Paul Drexel, rode up to the wagons and dismounted. The others were still with the herd, seeing to it that the animals remained settled on the night ground.

Hester had the fire burning, and was working with the cooking utensils. She halted, gazing at them. The first lowering intimation of trouble flashed into her mind. "Ain't Elizabeth with you?" she demanded.

The rising note in her voice brought them all swinging around to peer at her.

Abel answered, "She headed for the wagons a long time ago." He looked at the lingering glint of day on the peaks. "Half an hour ago, or longer."

He ran to his horse. The others were in the saddle a moment later.

In the fading light they found the sorrel Lisa had been riding. It lay dead in the barranca, its throat cut. A haunch had been slashed from it for food. Abel, looking at it, understood that this had been done while the animal was alive.

They brought brands from the cookfire and lighted torches of dry reeds. Abel studied the tracks. "She fought 'em," he said. "They might keep her with 'em for awhile. They like the kind thet fight back. The torture lasts longer."

They found Lisa's torn blouse and the deep heelmarks of her saddle boots where she had tried to escape. Some of her captors had been barefoot, some in moccasins and others wearing shoes or probably army boots.

Abel picked up strands of Lisa's coppery hair, along with coarse black wisps. "Might be Navajoes, or even Mojaves who could have been on a huntin' trip this far east. But the way they treated the horse says Apache. No more'n six to eight. But they might join a bigger party."

They returned to the wagons and got ammunition and rifles. Hester gave them what food she could put up in a hurry, along with filled canteens. Every man had come in from the herd, summoned by Abel.

"We can't afford to wait 'til daylight," he told them. "These Indians will travel all night to get out o' reach. All we can do is guess. They'll blind their trail, but in the long run they'll settle down to one direction. It looks like she was what they wanted an' they'd been waitin' 'til the right chance come along to grab her at a time just before dark. If thet's the way it was, an' if they're Apaches, then they've been followin' us, keepin' tab on her. Maybe for days. An' if thet's so then, by rights, they'll go back to where they started from. East. Thet's where their women an' the rest o' their bunch ought to be."

"Or maybe south," Paul said. "The main Apache country is south."

Abel mounted. "We've got only one guess. Mine's east."

Paul rode to his side. "You're usually right. Let's go."

"All we can do is try to be ahead of 'em by daybreak," Abel said. "They probably won't expect thet an' will only worry about their back-trail. The rest of you, fan out in pairs to the south an' west, an' be where you can see a lot of country come daybreak. If you cut any sign, use your own judgment as to what to do."

He and Paul rode into the darkness. Hester stood, helplessly crumpling her apron in her hands. She looked at the other men. "Will we ever see either of them ag'in?" she said exhaustedly. "Abel's all I got."

CHAPTER 19

Lisa stumbled along with her captors. She attempted to lag, pretending inability to keep up. One of them again seized her by the hair, dragging her along, and she cried out with pain. That delighted them. She made up her mind not to show them any such sign of agony again.

They reached ponies which had been left picketed under cover at a distance from the point of her capture. There were three animals, thin, pathetic beasts. In the faint light Lisa made out the United States Army brand on at least two of them.

There were seven Apaches in all. Lisa was thrown aboard one of the horses and clasped close against the odorous body of one of the Indians, and they moved out, with four of the party trotting along on foot.

Presently they split up, but afterwards the others rejoined them, coming out of the darkness like ghosts. This maneuver was repeated again and again.

The moon, past the full, arose, but heavy white clouds drifted in the sky and they rode in shadow for the most part. On one occasion, bright moonlight caught the entire group unexpectedly as they were crossing the open, brushless expanse of a dry alkali lake. The Apaches instantly froze, holding the horses motionless until the clouds shadowed them again.

They camped in a rocky ridge shortly afterward. Lisa judged that the hour was around midnight. She was yanked roughly from the horse. She was numb with the cold and with fear. She huddled against a boulder, her arms clasped over her bosom.

Even Apaches apparently had their physical limitations. They curled up around her, wedging her in so that her only path to freedom was by stepping over their bodies. They seemed to drop asleep swiftly.

She tried to escape, despite the odds against her. She waited, trembling in the increasing cold, seeking to be patient until she was positive they were not feigning slumber. Little

by little she raised herself, first to a knee, then to her feet.
She took a step over a silent form.

One of the Apaches came to his feet and struck her with
the flat of his hand. The blow hurled her against the boulder. He kicked her in the side, driving the breath from her.

He stood over her in a black rage. One of his weapons was
a double-bitted ax with a shortened handle. The blades had
been sharpened to shining edge. He hefted this wicked object, the thirst to kill rising in him.

He finally decided against it. He kicked her again, the impact numbing her thigh. He spoke something in his sing-song
tongue and settled down again in his crevice at her feet.

She dared not move again for fear of infuriating that savage mind a second time. She was fully resigned to death now,
and prayed that it would come with a measure of dignity.
She lay, gripped by mental torpor. She aroused dully when
the Apaches awakened. Dawn was at hand.

They lighted a wisp of fire, using gunpowder, flint and
steel to ignite the few scraps of brittle twigs. Over this they
scorched chunks of meat which they ate almost raw. None
was offered to Lisa. She did not know it, but the meat was
what had been cut from the horse she had been riding—torn
from the living flesh.

The Apache with the war ax seemed to be the leader. Evidently he had claimed her as his own prize. When they were
ready to move out, War Ax lifted her, threw her on one of
the ponies and mounted with her.

They rode away from the rocky ridge and Lisa saw that
their course was eastward. The Apaches once more split their
trail, three of them vanishing off to the south with one of
the horses. Lisa and the other four continued their eastward
march.

They followed the course of a wide dry stream bed, the
sand very white beneath the hooves of the emaciated horses.
The strengthening daylight marked out the pattern of scrub
cedar and willows that fringed the low cutbanks.

Two horsemen suddenly burst at full gallop from a side
draw to the left more than a hundred yards away. Guns
began exploding. Lisa screamed wildly as she recognized
them. Abel and Paul.

The Apaches, screeching, scattered. One, on foot, fell and
Lisa saw the spurt of artery blood from his throat where a
bullet had struck. He rolled over, got to a knee and lifted a
rifle, firing at the oncoming men, even while the crimson,
pumping flow was draining his life.

Lisa fought War Ax, realizing that he meant to kill her
with the steel blade. She warded off his attempt to swing the

ax, scratching and mauling with such ferocity that they fell from the horse.

He swung at her wildly as she frantically rolled, seeking to scramble out of his reach. He missed, and the blade glanced from a small boulder with such force that it was twisted from his hand and fell at Lisa's side.

Abel was riding upon them at close range. He had a pistol in either hand, but was forced to hold his fire because of the danger to Lisa. War Ax had a pistol in his belt. He snatched it out and fired. The bullet killed Abel's horse. It made another stride, then crumpled at the knees.

The animal's neck snapped as it pitched forward. Abel was thrown heavily clear. War Ax fired. The bullet missed, but it tore into the sand inches from Abel's face, blinding him with the spurt of grit that it cast.

War Ax thumbed back the hammer of the pistol to finish Abel. Lisa had seized up the ax. She stepped in, swinging it overhead, and brought it down with all her strength on the Apache's head. It buried deep.

War Ax reeled aside, the ax still clinging, and fell dead.

The Apache who had been shot in the throat was down and dying. The two surviving Indians were fleeing, but were still shooting.

Abel got to his feet. He was looking at Lisa and at the Apache with the ax in his brain.

Paul came riding toward them. A bullet struck him, fired by one of the retreating Apaches who had paused on the rim of the cutbank to level a rifle. Lisa saw the harsh spurt of dust where the slug had pierced Paul's shirt. He slid woodenly from the saddle, a blank look on his face. He tried to say something. He sat down slowly. From that position he pitched over on his side.

Lisa kept staring at the Apache with the ax in his skull. She began to jabber incoherently.

Abel came to her, caught her and turned her away. "Don't look!" he commanded.

"Hester killed one with a pitchfork!" she chattered. "I used an ax!"

She pulled away from him and ran to Paul's side. Blood was flowing, forming a spreading dark stain on his shirt. "He's gone, too," she mumbled.

Abel bent close over Paul. He looked up at her, then seized her and shook her violently. "Hang on! Hang on! He's not dead—yet!"

That drove the hysteria from her. Another bullet passed so close that she heard the crackling sound of displaced air. Abel got to his feet and began firing. She did not look up.

She stripped off Paul's shirt and saw the wound. The bullet had passed entirely through the flesh below his lower ribs. With strips from the shirt she stemmed the blood and formed a bandage. Abel returned and helped her. The two Apaches had pulled out.

Paul revived. He lay looking up at her. With an effort he brought a grin to his gray face. "Now you're a gorgeous sight to behold, fair lady," he murmured.

Lisa had forgotten how scant was her garb. Abel pulled off his saddle jacket and handed it to her and she donned it.

"I reckon the cuss ain't so bad off after all, if he can still admire the scenery," Abel said gruffly.

"The scenery," Paul murmured, "just took a turn for the worse."

"And so will you, if you keep talking," Lisa warned.

Paul was in great pain, a matter that he tried futilely to conceal. They glimpsed Apaches in the distance occasionally. Apparently the three Indians who had split off from the party earlier had heard the firing and had returned to join the two survivors. They hovered in the vicinity, seeking a position from which to get a shot at their quarry, or to move in.

Abel kept an eye on them from the rim of the cutbank, and used his rifle occasionally to discourage them from coming any closer.

Lisa remained with Paul. He insisted that he was able to ride, but Lisa overruled him for another hour or more. By that time the sun was well up, and the warmth of the day was making itself felt. Paul was obviously stronger. The Apaches were still around, and Abel was of the opinion that they might be awaiting the arrival of others.

Lisa helped him lift Paul into the saddle of his horse. Lisa mounted postilion with Paul and supported him with an arm around him.

"This," Paul mumbled, "is real nice. A little tighter, please."

Abel caught up one of the hard-used Army horses, which had remained in the river bottom, and mounted it. The other animal had escaped during the fight.

They emerged into the open, staying clear of gullies or outcrops that might offer a chance for ambush. They sighted the Apaches skirting their route to the south but keeping out of rifle range.

After half a dozen miles of travel, Abel pointed. The Indians had turned back and were heading steadily eastward. "They've give up," he said. "They figure another fight wouldn't be worth the cost."

Abel's mount gave out suddenly. He turned it loose and traveled on foot, occasionally grasping the stirrup or tail of the remaining horse for the sake of faster progress.

Paul was silent, but suffering. His wound bled at intervals, and Lisa called a halt often to give him a chance to strengthen.

"How did you ever find me?" she asked Abel.

"Mostly luck. We guessed they'd turn east. Aimed to be ahead of 'em, come daybreak. The moon helped us last night. We was on a rise near an alkali flat when the moon came out o' the clouds. We spotted the Apaches on the flat, pretendin' to be clumps of salt bush. Next time the moon came out, there wasn't any black dots on thet *playa*. When we didn't see any sign of 'em beyond the ridge in the moonlight later on, we figured they'd camped. We tracked 'em to thet arroyo this mornin', an' picked a good spot to jump 'em."

It was noon when they sighted the herd far ahead. Abel fired a signal shot. Soon the supply wagon, driven by Hester, raced toward them, accompanied by riders. The other men of the crew had returned from their futile hunts.

"I'm tired," Paul murmured, and began to sag.

Abel lifted him from the horse and held him in his arms. "He'll make it for sure now," he said to Lisa. "You an' Hester will see to thet."

Lisa gazed at this gaunt, unshaven, weary man who stood bearing his comrade's weight. Within her was a swelling, uplifting emotion. Abel straightened a little as though something in her eyes had lightened his own burden.

"I didn't kill Frank O'Hara," he said suddenly. "I want you to believe thet. Nor did Matthew." This was the first time he had ever unbent from his pride to voice a denial.

"Do you think I did it?" Lisa demanded.

"No," he said. "I never have thought thet."

They said nothing more, for the wagon was coming up fast, bouncing over the rough terrain. They kept gazing at each other. When they finally turned to greet Hester and the others, Lisa found the strengthening emotion continuing to soar within her.

Abel was right. Lisa, with Hester's help, saw to it that Paul made it. Once the shock had passed, he strengthened.

They remained camped three days and he recuperated speedily. When they resumed the journey he was better able to withstand the jolting of the hoodlum wagon, where he lay slung in a hammock made of wagon sheets.

The loss of time gave Kemp Travis an additional lead over them. Travis's herds, from the sign, were now some ten days ahead. But at intervals they came upon more carcasses of steers.

"What's his purpose?" Lon Melton asked plaintively. "Our

drive is contracted to Diehl & Diehl. What good will it do Kemp to get to Nevada first?"

Micah Jones was the one who answered. "Maybe he thinks we'll never make it."

CHAPTER 20

Full heat of early August gripped the desert as they descended from the mountains to the great river of the southwest, the Rio Colorado.

Lisa, remembering the Pecos, looked foward to this crossing with dread. But the Colorado was at midsummer ebb. What swimming water there was for the stock ran swift and muddy, but in channels that were easily crossed. The herd made it without loss of a head.

Lisa and Hester, with the wagons, found passage on a wagon ferry at a mining camp named Hardyville, a few miles from the cattle ford.

The river cast them ashore in a land harsher than any they had seen. The heat was of a kind they had never before experienced. It bore down on them like a weight, heavy and relentless.

Within an hour after they had left the stream, the cattle were uneasy and lowing. Mountain ranges, sterile and splashed with the furnace hues of slag and sulphur and copper, rose ridge on ridge around them. The soil underfoot was loose and without character. It offered treacherous purchase for hooves. Creosote brush and burro-weed thinly clothed the land. Cholla and deerhorn cactus speckled the higher benches, and higher up the grotesque Joshua trees marched with them like an army of skeletons, then fell behind as they descended to the glaring alkali flats where brittle salt bush fought for existence.

A few days of this and some of their own cattle began to die. Each day the number in the drag was reduced by a few as the weaker animals gave up. The Longhorns needed no urging now. They followed the herd leaders willingly, hurrying along as though in fear of being left behind.

"We're beginning to see why Diehl & Diehl are willing to pay twenty a head for Texas cattle," Paul said.

Desert spring, two days' drive apart, carried them through the mountains, but they emerged into a vast land with the interminable creosote brush stretching endlessly to the horizon.

Abel located a village of desert Indians who called themselves Cocopahs. For the price of a steer he hired the services of a guide. The Cocopah promised to show them waterholes and the way to the Mojave River. He led them a dozen miles deeper into the wastes westward, then vanished during the night.

At dawn Lisa rode ahead with Abel, scanning the desert for the water the Indian had talked about. All they could see was the monotony of alkali flats and benches and dry mountains.

They trailed ahead all day and with no appreciable change in the vista westward. Sundown came. "We'll have to keep 'em movin'," Abel said. "Maybe we'll hit this water by mornin'. It's moonlight tonight."

They had one other hope. August was the month of thunderstorms on the desert. Massive clouds had, in fact, formed late in the afternoon, and rain streamers had hung down over ridges far, far to the north. But the rain squalls had come no closer. And as darkness came the skies cleared.

The cattle marched along beneath the moon, expectantly at first because of the respite from the sun. But the land radiated the stored heat of the day and the hope of coolness was unfulfilled. Toward midnight the steers began to low dolefully. This sound became a moaning lament.

Abel called a halt two hours before dawn. A cool stirring of breeze had finally set in and the cattle sank down to rest, the moaning fading for a time.

Lisa lay on the pallet in the wagon, too tired to even take off her boots. But she could not sleep despite her weariness. She finally crept quietly from the wagon.

All the men were asleep—except Abel. He sat, touched by the glow of the dying fire but out of reach of its heat, his arms locked around his drawn-up legs, his knees almost against his chin. He was gazing off into the darkness, toward the herd which needed no guard to keep it on its bedground this night.

He became aware of her presence and his head turned. She moved to his side. She was silent for a moment, then said, "You must get some rest."

"Maybe I should have turned back yesterday," he said. "The cattle were still strong enough to have made it back to the Colorado. Now they can't."

"The word," Lisa said, "is 'we,' not 'I.' And it is not a matter of grammar. If there was any error in not turning back, you are not the one to take all the responsibility. We are in this together."

He got to his feet. "I stand corrected, Elizabeth," he said.

"You continue to improve," she said.

"In book learnin', you mean?"

She smiled wearily. "No. That is immaterial. You are learning you can't carry all the burdens alone."

His face was in shadow so that she could not perceive whatever might be his expression. "I can sleep now," he said abruptly.

"Good night, Abel," she said, and turned to move back to the wagon. He was still standing there watching as she entered the vehicle. And soothed, she fell asleep at once.

At sunrise they were awake and working to get the reluctant cattle in motion. Finally the animals were shambling westward again. The dawn was cool, but soon the sun lifted a molten eye over the rim.

By mid-morning the cattle were moaning again, and weaker ones were beginning to falter. The column of Longhorns began to stretch out to more than a mile in length—nearly two miles. More cattle began to fall by the wayside.

The heat was like a heavy, bullying hand on Lisa's shoulders. She rode bowed and spent before it. A steer, walking blindly, came veering out of the herd. Her horse, trained to oppose such straying, did not lift its head or move to intercept it. It was with an effort that Lisa kneed the horse into its duty.

A long time afterward, she became aware that the sun's assault had been interrupted. She looked up. A cloud, black-bellied with massive gray battlements, was moving in overhead. More clouds had formed over the mountains and were approaching! The sky darkened.

Paul, on point, rose in the saddle, his arms outstretched in supplication. "Dear Lord. Dear Lord . . . !"

The storm burst overhead. Lightning tore apart the blackness of the sky. Thunder struck in a cascade of sound.

The rain fell. Rain such as Lisa had never seen. She had heard men talk of desert cloudbursts. Now she knew. Rain fell in ropes of water. Rain that was like a suffocating torrent—and a benediction.

The moaning of the cattle ended. Lisa found Abel at her side. "Get in the clear, in case they start runnin'!" he shouted. He caught the headstall of her horse and led her to safer distance from the cattle.

But the Longhorns did not run. They moved ahead, horns glistening in the lightning flashes, backs sleek and wet and shining. They moved eagerly.

The storm rolled eastward and burst against mountains

beyond. The sun came out again. But gullies that had been skeleton-dry ran brimful for a time. Before sundown the desert had swallowed all this and the arid face was back on the land. But the cattle had drunk their fill.

"We'll make it now," Abel said.

It was late afternoon the next day when Paul, now almost fully recovered from his wounds, stood in the stirrups, waving his hat and pointing. They were emerging from a notch in the mountains. Before them lay a great trough in the desert. Near at hand, threading its way across the flats, was a meandering line of willows and cottonwood and patches of marshy grass. Water! The Mojave River!

The cattle caught the scent of the stream and broke into a lumbering trot. Abel joined Lisa, and they rode to accompany Hester and the wagons. Before they reached the river they came upon the forms of more dead cattle scattered in the dry brush. The animals bore the brands of Kemp Travis's drives.

Travis had reached the river, recruited the strength of his Longhorns for a day or two, and pulled out, following the river westward. He was still in advance of them.

"But only two or three days now," Abel said. "We're beginnin' to pull up on him."

"How far to this Nevada?" Hester asked wearily. "To this Reno?"

"A month's drive, accordin' to my maps," Abel said. "We'll follow the river a few days, then strike north if there's water to be had in that direction. We're in the state of California now, but Nevada bulges to the west an' we'll get to it by headin' north along a river called the Owens, which seems to follow a valley between two big mountain ranges."

Their present stretch of trail along the Mojave was much-traveled, being used by freighters between Salt Lake City and points in California.

At a freight station, Lisa listened while a bearded Mormon jerkline teamster answered Abel's questions. "Two herds, mister. Owned by a man named Travis. Texas man, like yourself, by his manner of speech, my friend. Passed by here the day before yesterday."

They were pulling up on Travis's drives. The Mormon also gave them information as to the route to follow after they left the Mojave for the swing northward to the Owens.

They were ten days on this leg of the journey. It was desert country as before, but Lisa felt its harshness diminish each day as they advanced northward. They found water where the Mormon had directed, and lost only a few more head of the weaker stock.

To the west, an enormous range of mountains began to bulge higher as they advanced, and another mountain mass came into view of the north and east. They were imperceptibly climbing to higher elevation and leaving the furnace-heat of the desert behind.

But always ahead of them was the trail of Travis's cattle. He was still driving hard, and losing steers. Their own herd was in fair shape, Abel said, and walking its fifteen to eighteen miles a day.

To Lisa, the nights when their herd had been stampeded on the Pecos and Abel had panicked Travis's Longhorns in retaliation, and the ensuing exchange of threatening bullets through wagon tops, seemed a part of a past that was over with.

A thousand miles of dust lay between those camps and the ones they now pitched. The saber-rattling, she tried to assure herself, had halted such strife permanently. Each side had found the other armed and determined and capable of striking back violently. It was, she had told herself until she almost believed it, a truce that neither would dare break.

But there were other moments when she watched Abel sit staring into the fire, a grimness holding him, his thoughts far away. A similar dark mood lay upon Paul Drexel on many occasions.

It was at such times that she knew in her heart that she was wrong. There was Matthew to remember. He was not forgotten. Nor was his slayer.

They reached the Owens, and the herd drank cold, clear water. The long drought had ended, but too late to save the native cattle in the parched ranges in the valleys west of the mountains. But the high country was greening again.

They trailed northward through a broad valley, shadowed by snow-streaked peaks. Settlers were in this country, and mining camps in the mountains. Rushing streams came down from the canyons, nourishing meadows on which the Longhorns thrived.

Around them the rabbit brush was budding, and some of it was bursting into golden yellow bloom. They moved through a land of beauty.

Paiute Indians roved this country, and stole two horses one night in spite of Shadrack's vigilance. But the Paiutes, in daytime, were wheedlingly friendly.

They left the Owens in favor of easier traveling through sagebrush country to the east. Abel said the Nevada line was nearby, according to the maps. They bore northwestward and passed a sizable lake whose surface mirrored extinct volcanoes. Its waters were mineralized and not drinkable, although fresh, rushing streams entered it.

They labored through mountains for two days, and emerged into a wide basin. A sea of lush green grass lay before them, laced with meandering streams. Pine, fir and cedar clothed the flanks of the mountains.

Lisa halted her horse, the grandeur of the scene clutching at her heart. Abel rode up and halted also, gazing for a long time.

Finally he spoke. "This, God willin', is where we'll settle. I never saw country so purty, never dreamed anything could be like this."

They descended into the basin and bedded the herd that night on grass that brushed the stirrups.

"A hundred miles to Reno," Abel said. "Less than a week's easy drive. An' this is the third day of September. We stand to beat delivery date by a considerable margin. Might come close to sellin' at twenty-three a head, countin' bonus."

At this altitude, as soon as the sun left the peaks, the wind brought the promise of winter. Lisa huddled close to the warmth of the fire that night as she helped Hester with the evening meal. Full moon had come again. Frost glinted on the weathered tilts of the wagons. Under that touch the canvas was all silver and purity. The stains of months of travel were erased by that magic.

Micah Jones lighted his pipe and sang:

> *"Buffalo gals, can't you come out tonight?*
> *Can't you come out tonight,*
> *Can't you come out tonight?*
> *And dance by the light o' the moon?"*

Nephi accompanied him on the mouth harp. Abel got out the books he carried in his saddlebags and resumed his determined study, a duty he had been unable to carry out in weeks.

Paul Drexel had Lisa trim his hair in anticipation of walking the streets of Reno town. He danced with her around the wagon circle to Nephi's music. They were lighthearted as they turned in for the night—for the first time since Los Molinos.

Lisa awakened and lay listening. Through a slit in the wagon flap she could see the morning star blazing brightly. A horse was moving somewhere near the camp, but the sound was so elusive she felt she was sensing it, rather than hearing it.

It probably was one of the men from the late watch, coming in to awaken the camp. Still . . . this almost inaudible presence seemed to be circling the wagons rather than approaching them.

She dressed quickly beneath the blankets, pulled on her boots and slid to the ground without awakening Hester.

The men were all asleep beneath their tarps. The peaks to the west were black, formless shadows against the cold stars. The air had the sharp, brittle chill of new ice. She could feel its sting deep in her throat.

She became aware of another shadow nearby. A horseman was halted just beyond the wagons.

She spoke questioningly. "Micah? Ygnacio?"

A sulphur friction match flared. Her first thought was that it was to light tobacco. She now discovered that two riders were there—vague shapes in the darkness.

The match burned steadily. Something new ignited. A streak of fire came sailing through the air into the camp, sparks flying.

Lisa realized what it was! She screamed, "Abel! Abel! They're trying to blow up the camp!"

The oncoming object landed a dozen feet beyond her and went rolling and bouncing, the splutter of fire continuing to burn balefully. This came from a lighted fuse.

She raced in pursuit of it. Her outcry had brought Abel and the others out of their blankets. The object rolled toward Paul. He leaped, seized it up, whirled and hurled it far over the wagon.

"Get down!" Abel shouted.

Lisa dropped flat on the ground. The earth seemed to lift and strike her with a solid impact. The concussion punched at her eardrums.

Abel squirmed to her side and dragged her beneath the chuckwagon. She heard the crash of descending debris.

That ceased. They emerged and got to their feet. The force of the explosion had flailed the embers of the fire into feeble life. Men were still crouched on their blankets, arms over their heads in attitudes of self-protection.

The supply wagon had taken the brunt of the damage. It was tilted on smashed wheels, its top blown off. Hester was huddled beside it, her face ashen. Lisa and Abel raced to her side. She was unhurt, evidently, but dazed.

Lisa became aware of a new, deep sound. The herd was running, panicked by the blast. The morning star was dim through a haze of dust thrown up by the concussion. The mounted men were gone. The rumble of the stampede covered any sound of their retreat.

Abel kicked brush on the fire and they had better light. He looked around. "Anybody hurt?"

Tom Zook spoke. "Come here, Abel."

He was bending over one of the men, the only one who had not gotten to his feet. It was Nephi Smith. Lisa started to moved to the place. Paul put out an arm, halting her, but she pushed it aside.

Nephi was dead. A rock had struck him on the temple.

Abel and Paul lifted him back on his blankets and drew a quilt over him. Lisa and Hester wept.

The stampede was a fading mutter in the distance. Evidently the run was already slowing down.

"There were two riders," Lisa told Abel. "I saw one of them light that thing and throw it. What was it? Powder?"

Paul answered. "Dynamite. I had never seen any before, but I know that it comes in sticks like candles. There were about three sticks. Maybe four."

"It'd have killed half of us if it had exploded in camp," Abel said. "They must have bought it at some minin' camp. Or maybe they rode into Walkerville last night an' got it."

Abel stayed in camp, waiting for better light. The other men rode away to overtake the cattle.

When the dawn strengthened, Abel picked up the tracks of shod horses in the frosted grass and followed them. Lisa caught up her horse and overtook him.

The trail led to a swamp stretch along a stream where the tracks had been swallowed by the oozy underfooting. Abel aimed for higher ground. They reached a vantage point as sunrise came. They pulled up there.

Far in the distance, perhaps half a dozen miles, two cattle herds grazed in the basin. They had been there all the time hidden from view by this ridge.

Two riders, mere specks at that long range, were nearing the wagons which stood east of the bedgrounds.

"One might be Coe Slade," Abel said. "Can't be sure at this distance. But neither is Kemp Travis."

He sat motionless in the saddle, his features hard and gray, studying those wagons. Lisa waited, knowing that whatever his decision, there would be no turning him from it.

Finally he swung his horse around. "We'll still deliver the cattle," he said. "Other things can wait."

He did not speak again until they were nearly back to camp, where the harsh fumes of the explosion still hung in the air.

"First Matthew, then Nephi," he said. "Travis ordered this thing last night. He's worse even than Slade."

They buried Nephi on a knoll overlooking the green valley. To his grave Abel made the same promise he had made to Matthew's memory. "We'll be back. This is where we hope to live. You won't be alone here."

The cattle had held together fairly well in the open flats, and by noon the riders had them bunched. The drive was soon in motion again, heading north.

The damaged supply wagon was abandoned. All of its necessary contents were added to the chuckwagon.

To the east of them, Travis's two herds came into view. Travis held an advantage of less than a mile. Lisa could see that he was carrying full crews with each drive. At least a score of men, not counting the cooks and wranglers.

Abel, for the first time, pushed their Longhorns. The men used ropes and quirts. The cattle at times broke into a trot. Travis's herds were being crowded to the limit also.

CHAPTER 21

Lisa soon discovered the reason for this race. The basin was walled on the north by a chain of rocky bluffs, broken only by a gap through which the trail led northward through broken ridges.

"If Travis gets into that notch first, he'll block us, or worse, when we try to pull through," Micah Jones told her.

But Travis had lost this contest many weeks earlier when he had weakened his cattle in the fast drive through Arizona and the desert. By noon, his herds had fallen abreast. By mid-afternoon they were dropping astern.

Lisa saw a group of Travis's riders gallop to the remuda and saddle fresh horses. "Abel!" she shouted.

Abel had foreseen something like this. He and Paul, Shadrack and Micah Jones were already changing to untired mounts. Hester came hurrying up with the wagon, and handed out rifles and ammunition. The four spurred ahead toward the notch.

Lisa watched Travis's men. He was leading them. She recognized his heavy figure. There were eight of them in all. But they had a disadvantage of nearly half a mile in distance. It was evident that their attempt to take physical possession of the gap was a losing one also.

Travis's contingent suddenly separated into two groups. Travis and three other men, one of whom Hester said was Coe Slade, drew ahead, but the other four had slowed their horses.

Travis and his companions finally pulled up and awaited the others. It was plain an angry discussion was going on. Eventually all of them rode back to take their places with their oncoming cattle. Their attitudes were those of sullen men at odds with each other.

Abel waited a few minutes to make sure the gap was not to be challenged, and he and his group returned to the herd. "Leastwise we separated the ones thet'll fight from the ones who don't think it's worth it," he commented. "We'd have been hard to handle if we'd got hunkered back of rocks in the notch, an' they knew it."

140

Looking back, Lisa saw that Travis was throwing off both herds. He had decided to bed his cattle in the basin for the night.

Abel pushed their drive ahead. Sundown was near as they mounted the long talus ascent toward the gap. They left the green basin behind and moved into a narrowing route that tightened for the last quarter of mile into a gorge with rugged walls. A stage and wagon trail used this pass.

They emerged abruptly into the open on a downslope. Open country stretched as far as the eye could carry in the purple dusk. The lights of a settlement glinted far ahead. Abel said that this must be a town called Walkerville, which was a supply point for mining camps.

They drove toward those lights. Full darkness came when they were still five miles away. Abel ordered that the cattle be kept moving. He took over the point and veered the course westward, at right angle to their former route.

He maintained this direction for nearly an hour before he gave the word to bed the animals. The site was an open sagebrush flat dotted with scattered pines, some of which seemed to be dead.

"No cookfire," he said. "Cold grub, if any, will have to do. No smokin'. We might have visitors ag'in. If so, we don't want to make it easy for 'em to locate us."

He ordered the chuckwagon unloaded. Working fast, he and Paul tossed out bedrolls and lifted food boxes to the ground.

"What are you goin' to do?" Hester asked anxiously.

"There's bound to be a store in Walkerville where a man can buy things," Abel said. "I'll need what money we got left in the sack, Mother."

Lisa spoke. "Buy what?"

"Corl orl, maybe, if there's any to be had in this country. Ought to be some in stock this close to the railroad. Or powder. Anythin' thet'll burn fast an' hot. Maybe even a barr'l of cheap whiskey, if I can't do any better. An' a few pieces of this dynamite, if it's for sale."

Lisa was puzzled. "Corl orl? What's that? Oh, you mean coal oil! Lamp oil. Now what——?"

He pushed past her. "Corl orl, dammit!" he snapped. "I'm gettin' right ta'rd of you correctin' me."

He spoke to the crew. "Everybody will stand watch tonight. But no circle ridin'. Spot yourselves at a distance from the bedground an' set tight. Shoot at anybody who comes near the herd an' can't identify themselves. If the cattle are stampeded, let 'em run. No matter how much they scatter, we'll find 'em sooner or later. It's you I don't want bunched up."

Micah Jones accompanied him on the wagon and they drove away toward Walkerville.

"What does he want with coal oil?" Lisa asked Hester.

"What would you do with it, if it was you?" Hester responded grimly.

Lisa stood peering into the starlight in the direction of the receding wagon. "Yes," she said in a small voice. "Yes, I see!"

"That's the way it is," Hester sighed.

Paul was stationing men around the herd. Lisa and Hester joined him, Hester riding a gentle horse sidesaddle. Paul placed them near a group of pines at a spot he believed was safest. They dismounted and tied up their horses. Paul left them, taking up vigil at another point.

They wrapped themselves in blankets. Even so, under a sky ablaze with pinpoint stars, Lisa felt the blue cold of the mountains penetrating with knife-like keenness.

Time dragged. She watched a meteor live its tiny life and flare out. Another burned brighter and vanished. The cattle stirred and arose, as though guided by a single mind, and began foraging. Lisa knew that this would continue for half an hour. Then they would settle down to sleep again. At two o'clock in the morning the maneuver would be repeated.

She and Hester found shelter among small boulders and sat huddled close together for companionship. Lisa had even dozed off when something aroused her. She started to her feet, the blanket dropping from her shoulders. Hester was already standing tensely.

Riders were approaching cautiously somewhere in the darkness. Hester held a pistol. Lisa also was armed. She drew the weapon. She was shaking at the knees.

A woodblock friction match spluttered into life. Again it was to be an explosion!

Hester gritted, "Blast you!" She fired. She fired a second time.

This lashback upset the horses of the intruders. Lisa could hear them crashing through the sagebrush. Hester fired two more shots, the powder flame darting into the night. In that flicker of light, Lisa glimpsed a rider half out of the saddle on a plunging horse that seemed to be tangled in the limbs of a fallen dead pine.

There were at least two more invaders, for two pistols were replying to the flashes from Hester's weapon. Lisa heard bullets strike brush and boulders nearby. She and Hester crouched down, hunting shelter.

"Ride!" a man yelled frantically. "Get out of here! Fast! I dropped the damned stuff, and it's lighted!"

That was Kemp Travis's voice. Horses were galloping away. However, from the sounds, the one closer at hand was still trapped in the deadfall.

Its rider screeched, "Wait! I'm snagged in——!"

That was cut off by the heavy flash of an explosion. The force of it drove Lisa stumbling back and she sprawled. She twisted around and covered her head with her arms as debris hammered down around her. A sizeable length of a tree limb struck within a yard of her. Pebbles and fragments stung her body, but she escaped material injury.

Someone was moaning in agony. The dead pine tree, ignited by the explosion, burst into flame, the dry needles burning fiercely. The glare lighted the scene.

Lisa screamed, "Hester!"

Hester answered. She was unhurt. They joined each other and stood listening, terrified.

The cattle had once again stampeded, but the run was northward and away from them.

As the rumble of hooves receded they again could hear the terrifying moaning nearby. They moved toward that sound. It began to fade, and when they were a dozen yards or so away it ended entirely.

Lisa forced herself to walk nearer. She halted, chained by horror. The ignited tree had expended its greater burst of fire, and the red glow it cast now was smoky and dim.

The body of a man was draped over the torn sagebrush, hurled there by the explosion. The mangled form of a horse lay nearby.

She heard the sound of wheels, moving fast. Abel's voice was shouting. He and Micah had returned from Walkerville. Paul was calling out also, and riding toward the scene. She had to try three times before she could lift a sound to guide them to where she and Hester waited.

Abel and Micah came running up on foot and Paul arrived and dismounted. Lisa pointed. She chattered an explanation and they walked ahead.

Presently they returned. Paul found the blanket Lisa had been using and walked back to lay it over the figure.

"It was a man who rode for Travis," Abel said. "They called him Red Leffler. He generally hung around with Coe Slade."

He stood lighted by the murky crimson glow. All sounds of the stampede had faded in the distance. "Well, we've got a spoiled herd on our hands for sure this time," he said.

He looked at Lisa and his mother. "You two should go into Walkerville," he said. "You'll be safe there."

Liza felt that she could stand no more. Nor could Hester.
Hester said wearily, "That might be best."

Abel and Paul Drexel caught up their horses. Abel held a
stirrup and offered his hand to Lisa. She accepted it. Suddenly she moved against him. His arms went around her,
drawing her close. He kissed her, questioningly at first, then
with realization and a full and growing hunger as he felt
her response.

He held her for a time. Slowly he released her. "We've
been a long, slow, stubborn time comin' to understand this,"
he said.

He lifted her onto the horse and stood peering at her in
the faint light, his fingers gripping hard on her knee. "Stay
in town," he said huskily. "Don't you get hurt any worse
than you have been in this damned business over these cows.
I can't lose you, too."

She bent and kissed him again. "What are you going to do,
Abel? I can't lose you either, you know."

"Stampede 'em in the gap," he said. "Travis will likely try
to rush his drives through as fast as he can get 'em movin'
at daylight. He knows we're scattered an' will be held up a
couple o' days or more. He knows too thet we've got a panicky herd which he can stampede whenever he feels like it.
He figures to pull ahead of us an' hopes that Diehl & Diehl
will cancel our part o' the contract if we don't meet delivery
date."

He added, "We've got some blastin' powder of our own
now. An' half a barrel of this corl—corl——" His tongue
couldn't master it.

"Corl orl!" Lisa supplied for him. "What else but that?"
She kissed him once more, very hard.

"Corl orl!" he said, and there was a vast tenderness in his
voice.

He headed her horse toward the lights of Walkerville, and
started it moving with a slap on the flank. She and Hester
rode side by side.

They heard the wagon begin moving southward. Paul
had joined Abel for this venture, leaving Micah with the
crew.

Lisa and Hester pulled up, suddenly realizing that this
was impossible. They knew what they would face in the settlement—questions, staring eyes, avid curiosity, demands for information. The explosion and the stampede would certainly
have aroused the citizens of Walkerville.

By unspoken accord they turned back and rode to overtake the wagon. Abel understood and offered no protest. The
four of them headed southward toward the gap.

When they reached the slope that ascended to the gorge, Abel said, "This is close enough."

Lisa and Hester remained there as the wagon rolled onward. They dismounted and found what shelter they could alongside the trail.

Chill hours passed before the sound of the wagon, returning, enlivened them. It was driven by Paul, and he was alone. The vehicle's contents had been removed. He left the wagon with them, took Lisa's horse and rode back toward the gap, a rifle slung in his arm.

The night was long. Occasionally Hester slept exhaustedly, her head on Lisa's shoulders. But Lisa could not sleep.

Dawn was in the sky when they arose and stood in the icy cold, listening to a distant and intangible murmur. Cattle were in the gorge. The sound grew in volume.

A red glow sprang into being. It rushed into fiery length— like the flash of the meteors Lisa had watched in the sky.

This ribbon of flame was in the mouth of the gorge, and though it was tiny at this distance she knew that it was kerosene, spilling down the walls and ignited by a torch.

The flash of explosions came next, sharply outlining the rock ledges and ridges. A moment later the dull slamming of the reports reached them. That was followed within seconds by the rumble of running cattle. This sound continued— a deep, sustained note.

Lisa understood what was happening in that narrow pathway. The first of Travis's herds had found themselves confronted by a barrier of fire. The explosions had added to the terror. The cattle had turned tail and the stampede had swept back through the gap upon the second herd. Some six thousand animals were jammed in the pass, struggling to escape by the way they had entered.

They heard the faint, lashing sound of gunfire. This went on for a time. Silence came, except for the continuing low mutter of turmoil in the gap.

First light of the rising sun touched the peaks. Lisa and Hester waited. Lisa found her mind empty, her thoughts formless. She saw how worn were Hester's features.

Presently Hester spoke in a thin voice. "Here they come! At least they're both still alive!"

A horse bearing two riders came out of the gray dawn. Abel and Paul were unhurt.

"They sighted us on the cliff and smoked us up," Paul explained. "But they only wasted powder."

Lisa and Abel stood looking at each other. Abel said to her, "It's right nice to be back. Mighty nice."

He gazed toward the gorge. The web of fine lines that had

been forming at the corners of his eyes and mouth since the start of the drive were etched more deeply.

"Travis is losin' a lot in thet pile-up," he said. "It was mighty bad. He'll never get the rest of the cattle into that gap ag'in. He'll have to take 'em east through the mountains into the sagebrush country. Thet's days longer, an' hard goin'. I doubt if he'll stampede us any more. I figure he's had enough of thet. He's got his work cut out, gettin' even three thousand head to Reno before delivery date."

CHAPTER 22

They returned to where their own herd had been bedded. Residents of Walkerville were on the scene, examining the site of the explosion and standing around the blanket-covered body of Red Leffler.

Like the citizens of Los Molinos, they were there mainly out of curiosity and had no intention of inquiring too deeply into the feuds and violences of these Texas drovers. However, two responsible men from the town agreed to take charge of Leffler's body.

"Kemp Travis will see that he's buried decently, or should," Abel told them. "He worked for Travis. You'll find Travis's herds in the basin there beyond the gorge, and he'll likely be with them."

They began rounding up their own cattle, which were scattered over a hundred square miles of territory. That task required three days of hard riding, for the run had been long-sustained, and many of the Longhorns had fled into the breaks along the base of the mountains.

They tallied the cattle on the morning of the fourth day. Abel sat shifting pebbles from one hand to another to mark each hundred head of animals as they were driven in a straggling column past him.

Lisa sat on her horse near him. She had a needle and thread, and placed a temporary white stitch in the cuff of her blouse for each hundred.

Abel counted his pebbles as the last of the drag plodded past. "I make it twenty-nine hundred an' forty," he said.

"Forty-one," Lisa said, totaling her stitches. "But you do real well at counting. Where did you learn?"

"Not with a needle an' thread at least," he said. "It's forty even, an' if I'm wrong, you've got the fanciest new dress you can buy in Reno as a present."

They drove northward again. Abel was right in at least one surmise. Travis did not again attempt to stampede them.

It was four days later and they were ten miles from their destination when Perry Diehl came riding to meet them, accompanied by half a dozen riders from Diehl & Diehl.

Perry Diehl stared incredulously from one face to another. His eyes rested blankly on Lisa. He did not recognize her.

Abel spoke. "She's a redheaded P'iute who's been taggin' along with us."

"Is it really you, Miss Randolph?" Diehl asked, stunned.

"I think so," Lisa said. "I'm not really sure."

The next morning she sat watching while the herd was tallied and delivered to Diehl and his riders. After the count was ended and the cattle were turned out to fatten for a time on grass, Abel rode up and dismounted.

"Go pick out that dress," he said. "Diehl & Diehl are payin' off on twenty-nine hundred an' forty-one delivered."

He added, "Make it a weddin' dress."

She sat looking at him, smiling, and within her was a soaring happiness. "If that's a proposal," she said, "it will have to be stated more plainly."

"Will you mar——" he began.

"Yes!" she exclaimed, and she kissed him. "But the wedding dress will come later. When we're in our green valley. This will be a party dress. Something gay. Something in which to celebrate, now that it's all over."

"Don't make it too durned modest," he said. "It wouldn't be fittin' to cover up all o' the purtiest gal in kingdom come."

"Your views have changed," she said. "You've learned more than reading and writing since we first met."

"Coal oil," he said. "It's easy to hogtie, once you get it throwed an' stretched."

She studied him and felt that his lightness was a mask. There was something that he and the other men were keeping from her.

"It is all over, isn't it?" she demanded.

He did not seem to hear that question.

Perry Diehl joined them. "I've engaged rooms for all of you at the Comstock House. And tonight you're to be my guests at supper. There'll be champagne. And more champagne."

At the Comstock House, Lisa and Hester arrayed themselves in the best of what finery they possessed and set out to amplify their wardrobes.

The herd had been delivered eight days ahead of contract date, earning a bonus of two dollars a head. Diehl & Diehl had paid in gold, the bulk of which was in a bank strong box for safekeeping. Sixty-four thousand, seven hundred dollars. Lisa's share, after the crew and other expenses had been paid, would take care of all of Frank O'Hara's debts. There would be little or nothing left, but she believed she was entitled to buy a little finery, at least.

"We'll live high while we can," Hester said. "We Barbees have gone bust twice in cattle. We likely will ag'in. Right now we've got money in our purses. I've always wanted a black satin dress. One that rustles real smart when you walk along with your nose in the air. I'm a-goin' to have me *two* of 'em, an' all the trimmin's. An' a real expensive bonnet."

Reno was a boom town and had stores with displays for feminine taste that were proclaimed as the latest styles from the east. Lisa and Hester plunged into the joy of a shopping spree.

They were trying on bonnets in a milliner's shop when Lisa suddenly became motionless, a gay hat trimmed with artificial daisies in her hand. Through the window she watched three men pass by on the sidewalk.

One was Kemp Travis. He was freshly barbered and wore new town clothes. His companions also were shaved and shorn and dressed in stiff store suits and collars. Only their darkly tanned faces told that they were just in from the trail.

All three carried pistols in holsters beneath the skirts of their coats. Travis's companions each had two weapons.

A desolation held Lisa. She knew now what Abel and the other had been keeping from her and Hester. They had known that Travis was in town.

One of the pair with Travis was thin and dark, with a hard face and very black eyes set deep beneath bony brows. He had a drooping black mustache. He was a stranger to Lisa.

The other was a powerfully-framed man with high, square shoulders. His features were heavy, almost bunchy, and his skin was burned darker than the others. Small knots of muscles played on his jaws.

There was something about him that was important, and she kept gazing at him. Somewhere she had seen him in the past and that was where the importance came in. But she could not place her finger on the time or the place.

Hester was also gazing at the trio, and Lisa saw in her face the same gray and chilling apprehension that she knew must be mirrored in her own expression.

Lisa pointed to the swarthy man. "Who is that man?"

"Him?" Hester asked dully. "Surely you ought to know him! You seen him kill Matthew. He tried to muss you up the time you was lost. That's Coe Slade."

Lisa stood disbelieving for a moment. It had been so dark she had not got a look at Slade the night he had tried to drag her from the supply wagon when she had been lost beyond the Pecos. He had been unshaven and in rough trail garb on that occasion, and also on that hectic day when he had shot down Matthew in Los Molinos.

This no doubt explained the impression of having seen him in the past. The three men were crossing the street, heading for shelter from the glare of the sun beneath the sidewalk portico of a harness shop.

"The one with the mustache is Coe's cousin, Jess Slade," Hester said. "He's a bad one, too."

Coe Slade looked back over his shoulder, as though sensing that he was being watched, and saw Lisa. That triggered something in Lisa's mind.

Her memory flashed back to that first afternoon at Monte Vista when she had been waiting for Hester to drive her to O'Hara House and she had wandered to a window and had noticed a swarthy, burly man walking toward the brush along the irrigation stream. He had looked back and had seen her—just as he had at this present moment, for he was the same person.

Slade evidently remembered also, for he paused in stride. Into his heavy face came a shadow that was hard and lethal.

Suddenly everything was clear to her. All the events moved into place in her thoughts.

She remembered the evening beyond the Pecos when she believed Slade had wanted to strangle her. Also the day in Los Molinos when he had looked at her over the pistol with which he had just slain Matthew.

And there was the night at Monte Vista when a bulky figure had stood near her, and had then moved away when Hester had called out. That had been Slade, and not one of the Bar B crew as she had assumed. She had been very near death on that occasion, as near as the night he had shot at her through the window of her room and later on had tried to creep in upon her sleeping quarters at Triangle O and had left Abel's horse and saddle as a blind.

He had tried repeatedly to kill her because he knew she had seen him at Monte Vista and that she might eventually understand why he had been there.

She spoke to Hester. "He's the one! He killed Frank O'Hara!"

"What? How do you know that, Elizabeth?"

"He was with Kemp Travis that day," Lisa said. "He

stayed out of sight while Travis talked to Abel and me while I was on my way to your place. Travis probably told Slade to follow me. He must have been listening outside the window to what I told you. Travis knew that Mr. O'Hara had met Perry Diehl and Major Gilchrist that morning. He didn't want anyone to talk to Mr. O'Hara, particularly you Barbees, until he had bought up cattle at a low price and clinched the contract for the six thousand head. Slade heard you say you were going with me to O'Hara House. That decided it. He had to act in a hurry. He couldn't take a chance on Mr. O'Hara telling you that cattle buyers were in the country. He knew of only one way of preventing it. He used a pistol."

"But how could Coe Slade have been wearin' . . . ?" Hester began.

"It wasn't a gingham shirt that he had on at all," Lisa said. "What it really was sounds fantastic. Hester, do you remember the apron you were wearing the day I first arrived at Monte Vista? Another just like it was hanging on the line. You told me not long ago that you had lost track of one of them. That stayed in my mind. Now I know what became of it."

"My good land!" Hester breathed.

"Slade saw his chance to turn suspicion on Abel, and stole the apron. He had it hidden on him when I glimpsed him walking away from Monte Vista. After he had shot Frank O'Hara, he merely wrapped it around him for a moment and let us get that look at him at a distance."

She quit talking and walked out of the shop and into the street.

"Wait!" Hester screamed. "Elizabeth! You can't——"

Lisa paid no heed. Travis and his men had paused in the shade of the portico. She moved into the open street toward them. They came to rigid attention, watching her.

She halted, standing in the blaze of sunlight, and spoke clearly, for she wanted neutral onlookers to hear the accusation.

She gazed at Coe Slade. "You shot Frank O'Hara. I know all about it now. You tried again and again to murder me because you were afraid that I would be a witness against you some day. You were right. That day has arrived."

She saw their attention shift slightly. There was in them the quality of the wolf pack. They had stationed themselves there for the kill. They meant to pay off for all their defeats, for all the cattle they had lost in the gorge. Their quarry had now appeared.

Abel was in the street. He had stepped around a corner and was moving nearer. He was coatless and wore two pistols. He spoke to Lisa, "Go back into the store, Elizabeth."

It was a repetition of Los Molinos. And again there was no stopping it.

Her fear for him was in her eyes, mirroring what was in her heart, but he shook his head. "They came here yesterday an' have been waitin' ever since for a chance to have it out with me."

Paul Drexel stepped into view and moved abreast of Abel in the street. He also carried two six-shooters in holsters. "I'm in this, Kemp," he said. "I haven't forgotten Matt. Nor seeing my parents scalped and butchered. That could have been prevented."

Lisa realized that both men were utterly remote from her now, living in a world she could not enter—a world of masculine anger and fierce pride and challenge.

A cold loneliness in her, she walked back into the shop where Hester stood, staring into the street. She knew her own features must be equally as waxen in hue.

Abel spoke, "Here's your chance, Kemp."

Travis evidently had not expected Paul Drexel's appearance. But there was no backing out now. He shouted, "Well . . . !"

He went for his pistols. It was Coe Slade who fired the first shot, however, for he was the fastest. The bullet struck Abel's left arm, the force of it spinning him partly around. But he stayed on his feet and was shooting back with one weapon.

All were firing. Paul was crouched, and seemed to be smiling as he fought. Jess Slade was hit by a bullet. He took a stunned step and slumped down on his hands and knees, gasping for breath.

Travis and Coe Slade continued to shoot. Lisa saw Abel stagger as he was struck by a second slug. Again he steadied himself.

Paul was hit also. The force of the bullet drove him reeling back against a sidewalk post. He braced himself there and fired both pistols at Travis. The slugs tore through Travis's body. He fell forward on his face, pulled himself to an elbow, trying to bring a pistol to bear on Abel. Paul fired again and Travis's head slumped down, his gun dribbling from his fingers.

Paul also slid to a sitting position, and then slumped over on his side. Abel stood over him, blood dripping from his left arm, which had been broken by Slade's first bullet. Slade was shooting at him, and missing. Abel fired twice.

Coe Slade was shattered by both slugs, and he fell along-side Kemp Travis in the street.

Micah Jones and Shadrack came racing to the scene, pistols in their hands. But the fight was over.

Lisa ran to Abel's side, Hester at her heels. She placed an arm around him, supporting him. He mumbled something.

Paul tried to talk but failed. Presently a doctor arrived. Paul was the hardest hit, but the doctor said that he ought to make it.

Abel's bullet-broken arm was an ugly, serious injury, but the second bullet that had found him had inflicted a flesh wound only.

Jess Slade would pull through. Coe Slade was dead. Kemp Travis was still alive, but he passed on while Abel's and Paul's injuries were being attended.

It was twenty-four hours before Abel, accompanied by Lisa and Hester, was steady enough on his feet to walk out of the room at the doctor's office that was used as a hospital.

Paul was still there. He was improving and reasonably out of danger. Abel had his arm in a sling and had a bandage on his ribs.

Perry Diehl and Major Gilchrist met them and walked with them toward the Comstock House.

"The champagne supper can wait until Drexel is able to attend," Perry Diehl said. "Is there anything we can do for you in the meantime?"

"There's a wide green basin about a hundred miles south of here," Abel said. "Water, grass, everything a rancher needs. If you can advise us how to go about gettin' title to grazin' land there, we'd be obliged."

"Of course," Perry Diehl said.

Major Gilchrist winked at Lisa, but addressed Abel. "You intend to propagate the land with cattle, I take it?"

Abel was smiling, his dark eyes warm and content. "With somethin' a sight more important than cattle," he said. "You know that, Major."

His hand was on Lisa's arm, holding her close at his side. Her fingers tightened on his wrist. "Well now, that's a noble and happy purpose," she told him.

Cliff Farrell was born in Zanesville, Ohio, where earlier Zane Grey had been born. Following graduation from high school, Farrell became a newspaper reporter. Over the next decade he worked his way west by means of a string of newspaper jobs and for thirty-one years was employed, mostly as sports editor, for the *Los Angeles Examiner.* He would later claim that he began writing for pulp magazines because he grew bored with journalism. His first Western stories were written for *Cowboy Stories* in 1926 and his byline was A. Clifford Farrell. By 1928 this byline was abbreviated to Cliff Farrell, and this it remained for the rest of his career. In 1933 Farrell was invited to contribute a story for the first issue of *Dime Western.* He soon became a regular contributor to this magazine and to *Star Western* as well. In fact, many months he would have a short novel in both magazines. Farrell became such a staple at Popular Publications that by the end of the 1930s he was contributing as much as 400,000 words a year to their various Western magazines. In all, Farrell wrote nearly 600 stories for the magazine market. His earliest Western fiction tended to stress action and gun play, but increasingly his stories began to focus on characters in historical situations and the problems faced by those characters. *Follow the New Grass* (1954) was Farrell's first Western novel, a story concerned with a desperate battle over grazing rights in the Cheyenne Indian reserve. It was followed by *West with the Missouri* (1955), an exciting story of riverboats, gamblers, and gunmen. *Fort Deception* (1960), *Ride the Wild Country* (1963), *The Renegade* (1970), and *The Devil's Playground* (1976) are among the best of Farrell's later Western novels. *Desperate Journey,* a first collection of Cliff Farrell's Western short stories, has also been published.